THE LOST BOY

S.A. MCEWEN

Published by Kaleido Text Media

First published in Australia 2021

ISBN: 9780648201397 (ebook)

ISBN: 9780645211016 (paperback)

Editor: Erica Russikoff, Erica Edits

Cover Design: Elizabeth Mackey

Disclaimer

For Lewis
A million times exceptional

1

———

The boy is gone.

His mother tears around the garden—the front yard, the back. Overgrown foliage scratches lightly at her skin as she bolts down the narrow passage along the side of the house, a first time, then a second.

Both gardens are empty.

She spills onto the street, a flash of color. Her red dress floats and wafts behind her, the material smoothing out the panic in her jerky stride. She looks like she is floating, not panicking.

The street is quiet and amiable, the warm spring sun a caress on her skin. A false promise, hinting at the impending summer: children playing cricket in backyards, parents sipping crisp white wine on decks in the bright Australian sun.

There is no one within sight, no cars to be heard.

A perfect suburban afternoon.

Except.

Her boy is gone.

2

SIX MONTHS Earlier

Olivia sighs deeply as she moves through the living room, her fingers lightly running across Nick's shoulder as she passes where he sits on the couch.

"That took a while," he comments, glancing at her, a question in his eyes.

She continues to the kitchen, rests her forehead on the fridge door.

Wolfie, their four-year-old, has stopped falling easily to sleep. After a bedtime routine that has been the envy of all their friends for his entire existence, he is suddenly clingy, anxious, teary. They've tried nightlights, extended cuddles, extended stories, extended play—trying to wear him out at the park after kinder—and eventually even ignoring him as he cried.

So far, nothing has worked. Exiting his room at ten past seven, with Wolfie already on his way to sleep, is a distant and ludicrously underappreciated memory.

Evenings cooking with Nick with a glass of wine, swaying to

some gentle music, and plenty of time to do some work or watch some television afterwards, likewise so.

Olivia glances at the clock above the fridge.

9.01 p.m.

Now, she's too emotionally wrung out to do anything. Nick has kept a plate of stir-fry aside for her, but even warming it up seems like too much effort. Partly it's worry—*why is Wolfie suddenly so anxious about things?* But mainly it's the result of parenting him without a break for what feels like months.

Months of someone needing her every moment of every day.

It's not true, of course. Wolfie goes to childcare three days a week. He's not with her all the time. But when he's at care, she's at work. Her days crash relentlessly between work, Wolfie, and the practical tasks of being an adult. Some days, even having a shower seems too hard.

Nick follows her into the kitchen, gently leads her to the couch, sits her down.

He heats up her dinner and pours her a small glass of the chardonnay she likes, then strokes her hair gently while she obediently eats and sips. The papers he was reading are pushed aside, his warm brown eyes focused on his wife.

"It's probably just a phase," he soothes her. "Starting kinder, having more time away from you. I'm sure you'll have your evenings back in no time at all."

Olivia nods. She pushes her plate aside and curls into her husband. Tucked under his arm, she breathes in the smell of him, resting her head on his shoulder. Finding comfort in his warmth and bulk.

At times like this, she thinks she's made a mistake. Nick is a good man. He thinks about her needs. He wants to take care of her. Of them. If she asks him, he'll do anything for her.

Her mind drifts back to the discussion in her lawyer's office. It seems almost ludicrous, now. Olivia often doubts herself, but this is an even bigger decision than all the other ones that stir her self-doubt. *What if she regrets it?*

What if she's lonely?

What if she's just plain wrong?

But nothing's happened yet. Well, nothing irreversible. Things have certainly happened. But she can snuggle into Nick's warm chest and pretend they're going to have a different future. Another child, perhaps. The wrap-around veranda they've always talked about. A bigger backyard. A view, even.

She closes her eyes and feels guilty. *Does Nick deserve this?*

The thought swings back the other way, though, as it always does.

Does she?

The papers are waiting. She could sign them, or not. She could bring down their house of cards, or not.

She could tear apart their little family, break Nick's heart, destroy their future.

Or not.

She sinks deeper into Nick.

She doesn't have to decide yet.

The papers have been ready for weeks.

She doesn't know why she doesn't proceed. She just needs to think. She needs to not be so exhausted, so wrung out by life. She needs a clearer picture of the future.

She needs to escape.

Or maybe she needs to fix things. Make them right.

She needs, at the very least, to make the correct decision.

But not now. Not tonight.

Soon, she tells herself. *I'll decide soon.*

From Wolfie's bedroom, there comes a low wail.

3

THE CAR HURTLES NORTH. Fast enough to get places quickly; not so fast it might warrant a second glance from a police car, patrolling the freeway out of Melbourne.

The boy in the back seat cranes his neck yet again, trying to see out the rear window. His long blonde curls are limp and unwashed. His dirty cheeks are streaked with dried tears. As he writhes again in the back seat, they start afresh, his little face crumpling, his breath hiccupping into short, shallow gasps.

Dark eyes flick to him in the rear-view mirror. He's strapped in too tightly to be able to move much; to see anything out the back window. Even if his little face did appear above his booster seat, a crying kid in a car is not so unusual. Kids cry all the time. The driver isn't worried.

The boy is worried, though.

He doesn't understand anything the driver says to him through his shock and tears; even if he did, he wouldn't be inclined to believe any of it.

He just wants his mummy.

He wants her now.

$$4$$

TUESDAY

At the press conference, Nick and Olivia look otherworldly. They've barely slept, barely eaten. Though Olivia has tried to apply makeup, her skin looks so pale as to be translucent. She wonders if the people on the other side of the screen can see through it into her thoughts, her being. She feels disconnected from herself, as though she's dreaming, as though this can't be real.

Later, she won't remember anything that she or anyone else said or did. The frantic searching of the day before merges and blurs into police questions and directives.

Did she knock on the neighbors' doors, or did police?

Information comes to her in fragments: Wolfie was not at the park. Not within a couple of blocks.

Did she search, or did someone tell her?

Find Wolfie, find Wolfie, find Wolfie.

It's the only thing that makes any sense. Food, sleep, basic functioning all seem absurdly trivial. Her husband, usually so steadfast and soothing, is as untethered as a balloon, offering her nothing to ground herself with.

There are questions, public pleas, updates from detectives.

There are people trying to help, dropping food off, participating in searches.

There are cards and well-meaning flower deliveries from the office Nick and Olivia share with dozens of other architects.

But there is no Wolfie.

$$5$$

WEDNESDAY

Nick is tying his tie in the mirror when Olivia stumbles out of bed to the bathroom.

She can't sleep. Her complexion doesn't cope with this arrangement; there are huge purplish-grey blotches around her eyes.

She stops in the doorway to the bathroom and stares at Nick.

"You're not going to work?"

The question is unnecessary. It's clear that that is exactly what Nick is doing. His hair is neatly combed, his shirt ironed. Even for the press conference he didn't make such an effort. The question is more to convey her disapproval, her disbelief.

Who goes to work when their child is missing?

Nick's eyes flick to hers momentarily, wary. "I can't just sit here," he says, his voice low, bracing himself for her response. But she can't even summon any energy to speak to him. She turns around, goes back to their bed, and lies facing away from him. Her eyes are open, her thoughts dark. Wolfie needs them. Anything else is a distraction, a betrayal.

A diminishing.

What could be more important than trying to find your child?

When Nick is out of the house, Olivia will rouse herself and walk the streets. Now, though, she lies stiffly in bed.

The police have told her to stay at home, in case Wolfie makes his way back there. They have enough people searching, they tell her. She suspects it is to keep her out of the way. She supposes they are more efficient when they don't have to attend to her wailing and grief as well as to the search.

But she knows Wolfie won't make his way home. He's four; he couldn't find his way home from a block away, let alone any farther. And a thorough search has established that he's not within a block.

He's farther. Farther away.

So far that she can't reach him. Can't help him.

She closes her eyes until she hears the front door click shut.

Then she springs out of bed.

PAUL EYES OLIVIA from the other side of his expensive desk.

It's Wednesday afternoon, and Olivia does not have an appointment. Usually, Paul would shoo her away, history or no history between them. He doesn't like his clients dropping in unexpectedly, but he has never quite made this rule stick with Olivia. He finds it hard to say no to her, with her wide yellow-green eyes and unflinching gaze.

Still, he's conscious of the minutes ticking by. He might find it hard to say no to her, but he's still going to bill her in six-minute increments, just like everybody else.

He waits silently. Impatience creeps out only through his hands—he moves some papers around, straightens them, tap-tapping on the sides until they're neatly lined up.

Golden light falls on the parklands opposite and below his generous office, the shadows already starting to lengthen.

"It's just not a good time, obviously," she says, licking her lips.

Paul notices the shadows under her eyes, the hollowed-out, greyhoundish look of her. Nervous energy practically rises off her like steam.

"Of course," he allows. "Nothing has been sent. The wheels haven't been set in motion. We can sit on this for as long as you like."

Olivia nods, one quick sharp nod. Her eyes are already sliding away from him, toward the door.

"You could have called," he says. "Someone might have seen you."

She glances back at him sharply, this new worry suddenly clouding her beautiful face. Even blotchy and grey, he can still see the line of her neck, her striking cheekbones. Usually porcelain perfection, today her skin is ashen. It pushes her from graceful and iconic into looking too thin.

"I needed a walk," she says, and slips out of the room without a goodbye.

The streets feel empty, though this is not in actual fact the case. The usual number of people move about their business. Cars honk, motorcycles rev. Conversations flow around Olivia, but her focus is narrow and in monochrome. Her feet tread one after the other.

She remembers just last week walking along this very footpath with Wolfie, noticing the changes, unable to be different with him.

Unable to be kinder.

Where once he would crouch every few steps to examine a beetle or exclaim over a pretty fallen flower or the shape of a leaf, now he's turned inward. In the fragment of memory, she thinks she can hear him counting under his breath, his fingers moving rhythmically to a pattern she can't catch.

WHEN NICK COMES home from work on Wednesday night, Olivia's face is deliberately, carefully blank.

At the work Christmas party where they met, it was his calm nature that drew Olivia to him. He chatted to her without any ego, wry and self-deprecating. The evening flew by, and Olivia couldn't remember the last time she had laughed so much and so easily with someone. Over the following months, he proved smart and kind and thoughtful. He never rushed into anything. He weighed things up, deliberately, sensibly. Reasonably. He seemed safe and reliable.

Tonight, these traits enrage her. His calm rationality in the face of disaster. His need to think first and act later.

He doesn't know this though. She keeps her face expressionless, observing her husband as though from far, far away. He looks so ordinary. It could be any day. It could be the week they moved in together. Or the day after his father's funeral.

Or the day after they lost their son.

When Olivia thinks "lost," she is thinking "misplaced," rather than "lost forever." But "misplaced" isn't right either.

There is something much more active about Wolfie's disappearance. Other words spring to her mind, but she pushes them aside.

Nick loosens his tie, glancing at Olivia as he opens the fridge door. Only she could see the assessment in that look. Thirteen years together, and she can read the nuance in a glance with indifferent accuracy.

Tonight, he's checking on her. Checking to see if she's all

right, but also checking to see if he's in trouble for being at work. For staying there all day.

For going at all.

Olivia keeps her face carefully neutral, and Nick hands her a glass of wine before he speaks.

"I've sorted out a few things so I can mainly work from home for the time being. So I'm ready to help, whatever comes up." He tips his glass up, swallows half of it in one gulp, and Olivia wonders about that uncharacteristic gulp. "I spoke to Detective Shelley today as well. Did you speak to him?"

She shakes her head, a tiny movement, putting her wine down, her hands against the bench, leaning in to it, her breathing audible. Deep and slow. The movement makes her look insubstantial, she knows. Feminine and fragile and in need of support.

She doesn't want to appear that way. But in this moment, she needs something physical and firm to hold her up.

Nick moves closer, slips an arm around her waist, presses his lips to her temple. "They'll find him," he says, and there's not nearly enough anguish in his voice to satisfy her.

What does "ready to help" even mean? That he'll be around to fix the sink if there's a blockage? Give Olivia a back massage? Join the police out on the streets?

She lets herself lean into him, nevertheless.

Later, lying in bed early—so early—she remembers the last time she tucked Wolfie into bed. She was exhausted, short-tempered. It was after nine, and she'd snapped at him twice already that day.

He'd taken to showing her how he was holding his fingers, the thumb pressed to one or two or three other fingers, seemingly random and nonsensical. He'd become hysterical if she didn't acknowledge it directly, looking into his eyes, though what was she even acknowledging? She'd learnt that what he needed was her to look at his fingers carefully, then look at him and nod. Then he'd seem satisfied, though Olivia couldn't understand it. At first it was two or three times a day. And then it was twenty or thirty. And over the space of just a few days it had escalated to every moment of the day. When he woke. Between each item of clothing he put on. Between spoonfuls of Weetbix and sips of his milk. When she was on the toilet, in the shower. While she was cooking or talking on the phone.

She had a nagging sense that he needed something from her that she couldn't provide. Did he need more attention? Did she look at her phone too much? But how much of your day were you *supposed* to sit, focused solely on your child? It wasn't realistic. It was demanding and dementing and *boring*. And was it even good for them?

"For God's sake!" she'd snapped, called back into his room for the fifth or sixth or seventh time. Nodded at his fingers. Kissed him on the forehead with unnecessary force, remembering a moment too late Brené Brown's words: "nice words, harsh face." Her kiss was a nice gesture, but how harsh was her face? Did Wolfie see it, in the dark? Did he feel it? Her rage, simmering just under the surface so often these days.

The memory of it takes her breath away.

What she'd give to kiss his forehead today. Softly, and with love. To see how he was holding his fingers. All day, every day.

Who was reassuring him now?

6

WEDNESDAY

Ray Smith pulls off the freeway and into the parking bay.

The truck groans and squeals against the empty night sky.

Out here, he can see stars to the horizon. It never ceases to make his breath catch in his throat. The expanse of it. It seems so...extravagant. In Melbourne, under the grubby smog, lurking amongst the crammed-tight buildings, such a thing was unimaginable. He was thirty-three before he saw it for the first time, and he hasn't gotten tired of it yet.

The familiar *whoosh* of the air brakes helps Ray to relax. It's the sound of machinery working the way it ought to work; but also the sound of security, of employment, of rest time. He tilts his chair back and half closes his eyes, watching for a shooting star. He likes to see one before he drifts off to sleep: it's his promise of magic, and beauty, and luck. He knows it's superstitious, but he carries some superstitions around with him relentlessly, unable to let them go.

Of all the things that he wishes he could let go of from his past—allowing to sink into the murky gloom of history, out of mind forever—his superstitious hunt for lucky stars is not one of them.

Two hours later, his alarm drags him out of his dreams. He blinks, a horn blaring, rising to a peak and falling away as a truck screams past him in the dark. Headlights blind him momentarily; some ass not lowering his high beams on the other side of the freeway. For a moment, his cabin is illuminated, and Ray reaches for his water bottle.

Next to it is the empty plasticware that had housed his lunch the previous day. Ray closes his eyes for a minute and thinks of his partner, fastidiously packing him something healthy at every opportunity. Not that it did any good—when he was away for a week at a time, he had to eat on the road. He did promise to go for the healthiest option he could find, but that wasn't always very healthy at all.

Now, Ray closes his eyes and wishes he was at home in his own bed. His partner would be fast asleep, though Ray knew it wouldn't have been easy to get to that state. He feels a pang of guilt, being away so much. Knowing someone relies on you, feels your absence so acutely—is on edge the entire time you're gone, even, waiting for you to return, jumping at dark shadows, both real and metaphorical—is a burden he carries every time he leaves home. Thinking about it makes Ray want to go home right this minute, soothe all those worries away.

Caring for someone might be the most important thing he has ever done.

At the same time, Ray loves his job. The hours of solitude. The horizon always so far away. Being on the road soothes *his* worries away. This is something that he can do, and do well. He looks after himself. He gets enough rest. He tries to squeeze in ten, twenty minutes walking every day. He has never once dipped a toe into the drug culture; he's been sober for eleven years.

Not to mention the pay. Deposited into his bank account

every fortnight. It's a miracle. It's *all* a miracle. The money, the job. Their apartment.

Love.

He can picture their home now. He can see how the whole day would have gone without him, right down to bedtime, his partner carefully marking the page in some hefty nonfiction book, placing it neatly on the bedside table, and switching off the bedside lamp at 10 p.m. exactly. The regularity of it never bores him. Each day, it's a miracle all over again.

Seeing this in his mind's eye now makes Ray yearn to be home even more, but the feeling soon passes, and a peacefulness settles over him as he starts the next leg of his journey. Because he, Ray, is doing his part in that picture. He is a cog in that wheel, and everything is moving like clockwork, as regular and reliable as his driving.

Their plans. Their future.

His partner might have designed the clock, but Ray is the one that makes it tick.

7

Thursday

Nick starts guiltily.

Olivia seems to have changed shape these last few days. Always slender, she now slips around him like a shadow, creeping up behind him on silent feet.

He shakes himself. *Creeping.* What sort of word is that to describe your wife?

He actually thought "grieving wife," but *grieving* is not the right word. "Grieving" speaks to something that can't be applied to them, can it? Their boy is missing. The police will find him. They're shell-shocked, and scared, and in pain, but they're not *grieving.*

Grieving is what you do when there's no more hope, right?

He glances at Olivia's face, trying to see how much she saw on his computer screen before he hit the close button, his finger hovering over the mouse in just the right spot for exactly this purpose.

He doesn't see anything there to alarm him.

Though she's staring at his screen intently, her face is smooth and untroubled. "What are you working on?" she says, still looking at the screen. He jumps on this topic, eager to show her his sketches and plans. Their passion in their work has always united them. It gives him something to focus on. Something that isn't the location of his son.

As he talks though, he can see Olivia's eyes going blank. She isn't actually interested. She has, in fact, recently taken her long service leave. Nick had been confused: it seemed such a waste. Why would you do that just to potter around at home? She'd even pulled Wolfie out of childcare for the duration. So even though she'd cited exhaustion as her reasoning, how did full-time childcare during your precious leave alleviate even the smallest fraction of that?

Now, though, he swivels around to face her, touching her elbow. She looks childlike, thin and ephemeral.

Lost.

At his touch, her eyes fill with tears, and he stands up to take her in his arms, grateful for the chance to comfort her. She's been so aloof since the press conference. Untouchable. He'd felt, suddenly—for the first time—that there was a whole other world behind her eyes that he wasn't privy to. The space between them had felt so vast, and he had felt unmoored. He's desperate to pull her closer again.

At that moment, she's everything that matters. The smell of her; the way her body melts into his, welding them together. Her remarkable yellow-green eyes. She's everything he's ever wanted, ever loved. Even in their worst fights, he's never not loved her.

And yet.

He can't explain it. If she is everything, why does he have Hannah, too?

***

"LET'S GO OVER IT AGAIN."

The detective looks at her kindly, and Olivia feels bad that she can't remember his name. She glances at his partner, Detective Rolands, and wonders why women's names always stick in her mind, and men's all blend in to each other, leaving her stumbling and embarrassed.

"Why?" she asks faintly. She doesn't want to be contrary. She just can't see the point. She'd wracked her mind for any detail she might have missed. Anything that might help.

"Sometimes it helps to go over it again, to jog your memory. In case there is some little detail you missed, that you see this time as you walk us through it."

Olivia thinks about that day, and her stomach tightens.

It's my fault, she thinks. *My fault, my fault, my fault.*

Wolfie is alone and terrified.

Or worse.

And it's all my fault.

But Nick puts his hand over hers.

"Is this absolutely necessary?" he asks. "Olivia has gone over it three times already. It's distressing, and to be honest, it doesn't seem like the best use of your time."

Olivia is both grateful and hateful. She knows Nick is trying to look after her. But she also thinks—*doesn't he comprehend that the detective knows how to run a case better than he does?*

"It's okay," she says softly, squeezing his hand.

Wolfie had been outside. Playing, she'd told the police.

She'd been in the kitchen, making cookies, getting started on dinner.

All that was true.

It just wasn't the whole truth.

Detective Rolands is looking at Olivia curiously.

"Why did you take Wolfie out of childcare?" she asks.

Olivia doesn't answer immediately. Why *did* she take him out of childcare? In retrospect, the decision was unhinged. She was barely coping with him in there.

Now, though, she presents the idea as she had presented it to Nick back then. "Something was wrong. He'd become so anxious. He wasn't sleeping, he wasn't playing. I thought he needed more time with me. It was so hard to leave him there. He'd sob. He wouldn't settle once I'd left. It was just heartbreaking."

She wonders if Detective Rolands has children. She looks middle-aged and tired. Despite this tiredness, her face is kind. She doesn't look like the sort of woman who would get snappish when life gets hard, who would let her own tiredness or frustration get in the way of being a decent human being. She looks like the sort of woman who could manage motherhood and work and family life without disintegrating. Olivia would bet she managed easily, in fact. Even now, with a missing child to find, with Nick questioning how Rolands is allocating her time, her approach is thoughtful, patient. She seems to have that kind of easygoing temperament, the kind that would roll with the punches and sort everything out. For a brief moment, Olivia feels a pang of regret—for all the times that she didn't roll with the punches. Where she did the opposite of sorting everything out.

When Wolfie would refuse to do something that needed to be done, for example. Like walk with her to the post office to pick up a parcel. His stubbornness enraged her. Hadn't she taken long service leave to spend time with him, without the pressures of work? To help him with his anxiety? To give him a good grounding for starting school? Just the two of them, moving through life at a slower place. Finding joy in the gardens they'd see on their walks. Trying to spot all the cats and dogs that peppered their route.

And then he'd refuse to go—or worse, sit on the sidewalk, his little face rigid with anger, the sun beating down on them. She couldn't cajole him, bribe him, engage him, entice him.

Usually, she'd have to pick him up, her fingernails digging

unnecessarily hard into the flesh around his tiny waist as she stormed home, her jaw clenched, rage bubbling inside her.

Why couldn't he just do as he was told?

She felt terrible afterward, of course. The shame of it. Losing her temper with a child, who was already riddled with anxiety.

But she hated him a little bit too.

Hated.

The word shocks her, frightens her. *Hated is too strong a word, surely?*

"Did it help?"

Olivia startles, pulled out of her guilty memories. She wonders if her face gave any of their content away.

"No."

"We'd arranged for an assessment with a psychologist," Nick volunteers. "He had developed some odd behaviors, a real fear of new situations. We were worried he wouldn't manage starting school at all."

"He was due to start next year?"

"Is," Olivia says softly, looking the detective in the eye.

Rolands stumbles her apology. But Olivia understands the slip. It's summer already. The new school year is only eight weeks away.

"But no," she goes on. "The following year."

Olivia has another month of long service leave. She had thought things would be better by now. That she'd be confident that Wolfie could return to kindergarten after Christmas; that he'd be ready to play with kids his own age again. She'd been so sure some focused time with her would solve everything.

Now, it seems arrogant. Delusional.

Did she help him at all? Or did she make everything worse?

All that time together. Wolfie anxious; her furious.

Like a four-year-old child could appreciate her sacrifices, her needs.

Olivia looks down at her lap, a flush of shame coloring her cheeks.

Nick continues talking, oblivious.

"His first appointment is meant to be next week, actually. We just wanted some more information. To see if something was wrong. Like, what does a four-year-old kid have to be anxious about? Olivia is a great mum. He gets a lot of her time and attention. He has friends he has playdates with. We live in a nice place. We just wanted to check we weren't missing something."

The united front isn't entirely accurate; Nick had thought it was over the top. "It's just a phase," he'd said to her at least a hundred times. He wasn't exactly a "tough love" kind of guy, but he didn't think ignoring the problem would do anyone any harm. "He'll grow out of it," he'd said, even last week, reluctant to take time off work to go the psychologist with them.

Olivia had bristled, her shoulders tensing to argue, to denigrate—*didn't Nick always opt out of the hard stuff? Didn't he always avoid those things that weren't convenient for him?*—but then she caught herself. She was secretly relieved. She felt she could talk more freely without Nick there.

Now, though, Rolands turns her attention back to that afternoon.

Olivia remembers it. Every last detail.

The smell of summer. The promise of good times ahead.

"I was baking. Usually Wolfie likes to help me, but he was being defiant. I said he had to pack up his trucks first, and he wouldn't. I got angry with him." Olivia's eyes fill with tears. She remembers his little face, shocked—frightened, even—as she shouted and slammed down the biscuit tray.

"He went outside to play on the trampoline. I saw him get on it. He didn't bounce, he just sat on it." He'd been sitting so she could see his profile, his legs stuck out straight in front of him, his fingers worrying at each other on his lap. He didn't look angry or sad. His lips were moving. He looked thoughtful, if anything.

Olivia had turned her back to use the mix master. Creaming the butter, adding the sugar. Her body still rigid with anger.

Why couldn't he just put his toys away when she asked?

Why couldn't she just stay parental and stick to reasonable consequences, without getting consumed by rage?

"I glanced out a couple of times. He was still sitting on the trampoline, in the same spot. So I rolled out the biscuit batter. I cut the biscuits out with a glass, put them in the oven. Then I went to the toilet before going out to join him."

In the bathroom, though, she had just stared at herself in the mirror. Took some deep breaths. Reminded herself that this was her job. To parent her child. And this was Wolfie's job—to be a kid and learn and push boundaries and stomp his little feet. She had to remember to breathe, to not get angry.

It was ludicrous, really. She was not an angry person. She didn't shout and carry on when things were unfair. Life could be unfair; she would shrug and get on with it. Work with what she had. Be generous with perspective-taking. Not take things to heart.

That was with other people, of course. She had higher expectations of herself. A perfectionistic streak she found hard to shake. An almost obsessive need to get things right. Which made her temper with Wolfie even more confusing. *Surely this was the most important thing she would ever need to be good at?*

"And he wasn't on the trampoline?" Rolands prompts her. "How long was it since you last checked on him?"

"I've told you. I really couldn't say. Maybe five minutes? Maybe more."

"And then?"

"I walked out the back door. I wasn't worried at first. He likes to dig about in the garden. He knows he's not allowed into the shed, but sometimes he goes in there and might hide if he hears me coming. I wandered a bit. I enjoyed the sunshine. I peeked around bushes like we were playing hide-and-seek. But when I didn't see him, I started calling out. I looked in the shed. I started worrying. That he'd wandered onto the road. He knows not to go out the front but he's four, you know? Maybe he was chasing a bird or something and forgot. I started jogging along the side of the house, calling for him. I went out the front, and looked over the fence onto the road. Then I went back around the back, thinking he must have heard me and gone down the other side of the house. To pretend he was never out the front. Because he wasn't out the front. And he wasn't on the road. So where else could he be?"

Olivia starts to cry quietly.

Her baby. Her dear little boy.

What had she done?

8

———————

Hannah stretches out her legs and rests them on the lip of the bath, admiring the curve of her calves, her perfect red toes.

She's always liked her feet. They're shapely, womanly. Her toes are perfect. She has no qualms telling her lovers to suck them.

She should be at work, but she's taken the day off.

With nothing to do, nowhere to be, her fingers wander almost mindlessly between her legs.

Boredom wank, she thinks. Surely she could come up with something better to do with her day off?

She wonders what Nick is doing. Men never cease to amaze her. Despite a missing child, he'd pulled off a pretend "work day" to spend some time with her, the clues not even cold on the ground. And though he'd been a bit more needy than usual, he'd still managed to come three times before showering thoroughly and heading to the office to pick up his alibi.

Her fingers pick up their pace, remembering that last time, up against the bathroom door. The way he manoeuvres her. His confidence that he knows what she likes and can give it to her without asking. Six months in, and they're still breaking furniture.

She closes her eyes, not bored anymore.

An hour later, still horny, she films herself masturbating, emails it to Nick. She likes the thought of being in his house, getting him hard, watching her furtively in the bedroom or the bathroom while Olivia is oblivious in another room.

Oblivious Olivia.

Honestly. Women trust men too much. She once had a friend whose married lover skipped out of hospital after the birth of his first child for a quickie, while he was "buying supplies." The affair fizzled out after that. It was too much, even for Liz.

It's not that she hates Olivia. If anything, she feels sorry for her. She also thinks that, if she wanted to, she could move Nick into her house without too much trouble at all. There was something about her that drove men crazy. She'd known it since she was barely a teenager, and had harvested it in her favor ever since.

Did she want a full-time boyfriend, though? Especially a cheating, lying one? Sometimes, though she'd never admit it, Hannah really did crave the normalcy of a committed relationship. And Nick certainly knew how to look after her, in bed and out. But she'd always valued the fun of new flings, new lovers. Finding them. Winning them over.

Longevity in a relationship did not seem like something she'd excel at.

But now, well. Things were getting a bit sticky. She'd put some things in motion, carelessly. Recklessly. She'd asked for things that she wasn't even sure she wanted. She was better at starting things than sticking with them. Or even stopping them, when the situation called for it.

She needed to think about Nick and think about her future. What did she *actually* want?

At least she didn't have to think about the child, now.

At least the child was out of the picture.

9

———

In his side mirror, flashing red and blue lights make Ray's heart jump into his throat.

Instinctively he pulls his knees upward, and the truck sighs and groans, it's momentum tanking against the steady climb immediately, reminding Ray to keep his foot on the pedal.

His heart hammers in his chest, but the patrol car speeds past him, lights with no siren. Within minutes it is out of sight.

Ray's shoulders relax, and he turns on the radio, smiles to himself. Soon, he'll see the river flats spreading out in front of him, the towering red gums making his heart sing. Who knew such a thing existed, just a short drive outside his hometown?

Would his life have been different, if he'd run outward, toward this, instead of further in?

His mind skips away from this thought, though. He knows he should sit with it. He can still remember Mandy, his case worker—her enthusiasm, bouncing right back after every put down, every crappy thing they said to her. God, she must have been straight out of university. He wonders what she made of her job. A whole bunch of juvie crims, her barely older than any of them.

"Sit with that feeling," she'd say, nodding encouragingly, when Ray tried to talk about that day. The day that changed everything. His father. His mum. Even now, he winces when he thinks "mum." But how could he talk about that? Mandy wanted to find their soft parts. She wanted to help them connect to something different to the hardship, the pain. The anger. She wanted to support the parts underneath. Their soft underbellies.

But life had never been kind to those.

Best to keep those parts hidden away.

Still, he wondered if he'd be where he was now without those conversations. It was hard to share those parts of himself in detention. But did they help him later, in his relationship? He's certainly found an intimacy he could never have imagined in those early days.

Now, Ray lets the landscape wash over him, rub off on him. It's the same one he saw yesterday, but he's learnt to be patient with other people's errors. He drives his truck where he's told to drive it. It wastes his time, when there's errors, and time *is* money when you're driving trucks. But getting angry doesn't help.

He glances down at his wrist. *Breathe,* it says, in typewriter font. It's hidden amongst other tatts, that have other meanings. But breathing to calm himself is something that he did take from his time with Mandy, and he's grateful for it. So grateful he had it inked onto his wrist.

Further up, there's a tattoo of a woman's face, a birth date, a death date. Most days his eyes linger on that, at some point. But not now.

He wonders what Mandy's up to nowadays. She was so optimistic every time he left, but she never chastised him every time he bounced back. She just got straight back to work. She was like Robin Williams in *Good Will Hunting*. She never said it, but Ray felt it. He could see it in her eyes, even in that first meeting, when he was so angry and rude.

It's not your fault.

It's not your fault.

It's not your fault.

But who's fault was it, then?

Was it his father's? Because you could certainly say that what his father did was the start of when it all went wrong for Ray. But should you go further back?

Why was his dad like that?

Why did his mum not see it?

Ray squeezes his eyes tightly shut, just for a second. He's trying to stop the memories; he knows these thoughts don't give him any answers, let alone any relief. But sometimes, on long drives, they bubble away, and he picks at them, relentless. It's harder to intervene, to redirect himself when he's just sitting in a truck, with hours and hours ahead of him, just him and his thoughts.

Now, though, another police car announces itself, the lights bouncing off his mirror and elbowing their way into his memories. He doesn't question the panic, though it's been years since the flashing lights have been for him. Panic is just the way it is.

Which cop will you get today?

Good cop? Bad cop?

The devil?

He shrinks in his seat a little. He knows he is safe; he knows he is a citizen of this country with every right to be on the road.

But his body remembers something different.

10

Five Months Earlier

"It's not like you actually spend any time with him."

Olivia leans against the door frame, her chin jutting out in that aggressive way it does when they disagree and she wants Nick to capitulate.

"I spend plenty of time with him. He's just not the only thing in my life," he counters, his voice even. He doesn't really understand Olivia's agitation. Wolfie is a handful, but he's not getting any worse. Privately, he thinks Olivia is overly focused on him, reading worries where there aren't any. His natural tendency is toward more discipline; he thinks Wolfie has Olivia wrapped around the proverbial little finger. Even this morning, Wolfie insisted Olivia be the one to help him get his breakfast; when Nick tried to insist that Nick, too, was perfectly capable of getting some damn Weetbix into a bowl, the crying had been ridiculous. And Olivia had tried to negotiate, tried to solve it, instead of just letting the kid go hungry, as Nick would have done.

"A four-year-old child shouldn't be so worried about life."

"That's true," Nick agrees, his voice soothing. "But we

should be just doing normal family things. We shouldn't make our whole weekends revolve around him. He'll settle. He'll get used to things. It's just a phase he's going through."

At one point, Nick thought Olivia might take over the world. She had the ability to see the big picture when everyone else was caught up in the details. At work, at leisure, socially, all of it. She had big ideas, big passions. She'd started the social club at work, the industry e-magazine, the running club. And these weren't just things to do—they were projects in inclusion. She could see gaps, she could see how to engage people who were struggling, she could just somehow coalesce a hundred smaller parts into something meaningful and magnificent. His workplace was happier, better, more alive because of Olivia.

Somehow, he thought that parenting had diminished her.

Now, all she thought about was Wolfie.

Of course he loved Wolfie. Of course he did. *But a child should fit into your life, not the other way around. Right?*

And now she was talking about splitting their family up. A country house for her and Wolfie, and a city pad for him to stay at during the week. The thought of not seeing either of them during the week is weirdly polarizing. On some level he feels relief: it would be so peaceful.

On another level he feels panicked: that Olivia would get used to life without him. Might *prefer* it, even. And maybe their lives weren't perfect, but that just seemed like admitting failure. Just letting it happen. Just giving up.

"It will be better when he starts school," he tries again. "When he has friends and a routine. When he's learning interesting things." Privately, he does think such a nervous child is going to be a prime target for bullying, but they have eighteen-odd months between now and then. Nick is a great believer in letting things sort themselves out. He wants Olivia to just leave it be, but he knows his wife better than that. She's not happy unless she's doing something. She's never been able to sit still.

"Are you wanting to split up?" he asks suddenly, his throat tightening. He might have Hannah, but that's just poor self-control.

Olivia is the one he loves.

She shakes her head, but without conviction. She looks restless. It doesn't seem to occur to her to pursue why Nick would think that, or comfort the thought away. "It's just so much cheaper in the country. I could take a few years off work, just be a mum till Wolfie is more settled. It's quieter. Sometimes the city makes my head hurt."

"Having two houses isn't going to be cheaper."

Olivia starts. *Did she really not think about that?* Nick wonders. Perhaps all the late nights settling Wolfie are getting to her more than he thought. He studies his wife more closely. There are purplish strokes under each eye, as though someone has roughly painted them on with a brush. The sparkle has gone from her eyes. Her posture is slumped, unusual for Olivia; usually she has an easy gracefulness, moving through space with effortless elegance.

Nick feels a pang of guilt. He hasn't been paying as much attention.

"Why don't we just take a holiday?" he suggests, gentle, beckoning Olivia over, pulling her slight frame onto his lap, nuzzling her neck, breathing in the smell of her. "We can go somewhere quiet and peaceful, just hang out for a while. As a family."

"That sounds nice," Olivia murmurs, leaning into him. He loves the feeling of it—like she's molding herself into him. Like she needs him so much she wants to become him.

Already, he is skipping ahead to solutions and fixes: where they could go, what would help Olivia to relax. The things that she might need that she herself is oblivious to. Sometimes, Nick thinks of Olivia like an automated machine—one that you set and forget and it just keeps going. She sets off with precision in one direction, finely attuned to her environment, carefully observing and assessing the requirements. But since they had Wolfie, it's like her focus then shifts to the action itself: the whirring, beating, mixing, moving, oblivious to whether the job is done or the circumstances have changed.

Without him around to temper her, he thinks she might just work herself into the ground.

Now, he throws himself into the task of finding them a resort for a week or two. It's an easier task to focus on than understanding the nuances around why Olivia might want to move to the country without him. In his practical way, the problem to solve seems to be a linear one—starting with spending quality time together, and helping Olivia get some more rest. Everything else, Nick thinks, will flow on from that. Better sleep. More optimism. More joy in the daily activities of living with Nick and Wolfie.

He books ten days in Port Douglas, with a swim-out pool and a day spa. He books Olivia a couple of massages, and books a babysitter for two nights, so he can take her out for some nice dinners.

He plans all sorts of ways he can help her to feel better, and goes ahead and books them, as a special surprise.

"You're making it shit, aren't you?"

Olivia startles, and looks back at Jodie sharply.

"It *is* shit," she says.

Jodie pauses when Maggie runs over. She pulls her daughter onto her lap and kisses her head, then pops her back down and pushes her gently back toward the trampoline, where Wolfie is bouncing happily.

"I haven't seen Wolfie this relaxed for ages," Olivia muses, thinking again about his rigid little face at bath time the night before. She had helped him undress, not thinking, and directed him to the toilet next to the bath. What followed was heart-wrenching. He had demanded she dress him again; he "did wee-wees BEFORE undressing." Olivia had refused, tired of his rigid routines, his inflexibility. Just tired, in general. She thought he would capitulate. She felt the familiar rage rising in her chest.

Just fucking take a leak, she screamed on the inside.

When he refused, she tried to manhandle him into the bath, the rage overflowing, like it did more and more these days. She was only brought back to earth by the absolute terror his little face betrayed.

He wasn't being stubborn or difficult.

Shocked, ashamed, Olivia sees that bathing out of routine upended his world to such a degree that he literally could not cope with the disruption.

Today, though, he bounces with Maggie as though he has no cares in the world. A little younger than him, they've known each other since birth; Olivia and Jodie have known each other nearly since *their* births.

"Don't think we're not coming back to this," Jodie warns, but follows the change in topic: "Has it been any better?"

"Not really." Olivia turns to face Jodie, dragging her eyes away from the rare sight of her content child reluctantly. "I'm asking around about a child psychologist. All the ones people recommend have wait lists months long." The thought both comforts and bothers Olivia. Partly, she thinks she knows her child best—shouldn't she be able to understand him, work out what's wrong? But partly, she longs to hand over the uncertainty and worry to someone else. "It's really like a matter of life and death to him, if something is unexpected, or out of his routine. It's not like a temper tantrum or a power struggle. At least I don't think it is. It looks to me like sheer terror."

Jodie clucks sympathetically. They have traversed the highs and lows of childhood, adolescence, careers, and now parenting together. There are barely any thoughts either has that the other doesn't hear about or guess.

Jodie waits. Olivia's brain whirs haphazardly, trying to find somewhere to land that makes sense, that explains how she feels. Eventually she offers: "I just don't feel like I'm very good at it. Parenting. I can't stay calm. I feel rage. Tsunami-like rage. I just want him to do what he's supposed to do. And when he's so difficult, I..."

Jodie nods encouragingly.

"I want to punish him," Olivia whispers.

She doesn't say the rest: that she does, sometimes.

That she pinches him a little as she buckles him, finally, into his car seat, an hour after they were supposed to head off. Or takes satisfaction in throwing his favorite treat into the bin as a consequence for something completely unrelated that he cannot understand. She knows it doesn't help. But it makes her feel better, for a little while.

Later, Jodie returns to Nick.

Olivia's lip curls involuntarily.

She doesn't want to talk about how she is or isn't making things shit with Nick.

11
___

"COME HERE, BOY."

The voice echoes out from a dark corner. The boy squints to see the furthest recess of the protection afforded by the bridge.

He doesn't know where he is or even how he got there. He does know that it is surprisingly quiet. Muffled sounds drift down from above him, but the pitch of them is soothing, rather than anxiety-provoking.

He had thought he was alone. He's cold and hungry, and had crouched down against a brick wall, the vibration of cars thrumming comfortingly against his back.

He had crouched down there, and had no further plans about what to do next.

He peers again into the darkness.

"Over here," says the voice.

The boy takes a tentative step toward it. His apprehension works in step with his hopefulness: that from the direction of the voice there might also come comfort. An adult who knows what is happening and how to fix it, perhaps. Even though adults have not proven to be terribly proficient in that regard, so far.

He can't think about the man in the car. He will not say his *name. He will not call him anything else but That Man. And he certainly can't think about what happened before the car ride. He has learnt what happens when his mind drifts back that way. To softness and biscuits and cuddles and—*

Stop.

He can't go back there.

And he doesn't know where else to go.

Again, the voice beckons him. "Over here. Don't be afraid."

He doesn't know what else to do.

He takes another step into the darkness.

"That's it, boy. This way. I've got something for you."

He's old enough now to wonder about how safe a man hiding under a bridge might be. But at just eleven, he's not old enough to come up with a better solution. And besides, nothing has felt safe for quite some time. Memories of breaking glass—a shower of it, glinting and spraying and twisting in the light, suspended in an arc out from the front door—and running, running, being pushed, panicked, are already getting buried, pushed down, far away.

They'll creep into his nightmares for years, and years. But right now, all he can imagine is food. Might the something be food?

His steps are tentative, not because he is afraid, but because he can't see.

One foot in front of the other, into the dark.

12

———

Charlie inserts himself into the room with his usual sense of entitlement.

It's not really entitlement, Olivia knows that. He's just a kid; they're all entitled at his age.

She bristles a little more than usual as he starts pulling various items from kitchen drawers. "I'm going to make ice cream," he says, to no one in particular, and Olivia wants to scream. When did he become so comfortable just waltzing in and out of her kitchen?

She takes a deep breath. He's lost his mother. Patricia is dead, and Olivia and Nick are the only family left that count. *Be generous,* she thinks to herself.

She had wondered, earlier, when her thinking was clearer, what Charlie made of the money his mother left to Wolfie; if he knew. She hadn't been worried that he'd mention it to Nick: Charlie would not think to be jealous or curious or anything else.

The phrase "self-absorbed" flashes in Olivia's mind, again.

"How are you finding living here?" she asks, swallowing her

frustration. Rearranging her face into something she hopes is warmth and interest. It's easier, in this moment, to pretend that their biggest challenge is how Charlie is settling in, than to let Charlie see her pain and grief and terror. Detached, it surprises Olivia that she is capable of such a question.

Now fifteen, they've barely seen Charlie over the last few years. Nick's son from a previous relationship, Olivia remembers him as old beyond his years. He made strange company. And though Nick had shared custody up until Wolfie was born, she couldn't say that she was sorry when Patricia, Nick's ex, moved to London for work. They'd barely kept in touch. Phone calls at Christmas. Birthday cards with hastily written updates and the odd photo. Nick had had him so young, and while he, of course, kept in better contact, Olivia had somehow managed to resolutely forget that he was a part of their lives.

Yet here he was. Patricia was gone barely three months, his half-brother was missing, and Charlie was making ice cream in her kitchen.

"Very nice, thank you," Charlie says politely. "I'm looking forward to starting school in the new year."

Olivia grinds her teeth and looks away. Nick, of course, has rolled with the punches. But for all Patricia's wealth, she and Nick will see nothing for their taking Charlie in.

It's the right thing to do, she had argued with herself. But she hadn't thought it through. She hadn't kept in touch with him enough to share a space with this boy. He was a stranger, filling her house with adolescent boy smells and adolescent boy inconveniences. His very presence grates on her nerves. The blank way he looks at her when she explains how things work or family expectations. The secretive little smile when she gently tries to correct behavior she doesn't want to see repeated. Like the time she left him alone with Wolfie for just a few minutes, and came back to a standoff—Charlie insisting Wolfie put his dirty plate on the sink, pulling him roughly by the arm, saying, "I think you WILL clean up your mess." Wolfie was shouting "*No!*" and resisting, his little face stubborn and angry. Olivia redirected Charlie, trying to conceal the flash of anger she felt, and asked him—again—to call her if a parenting task was required. "You don't need to do any parenting," she told him, half reassuring, half chastising, then turned back to Wolfie: "When you've put your plate away, then we can start that puzzle you wanted to do," she said, and walked away.

But Charlie's expression stayed with her, unsettling her. It wasn't a look of anger, but he wasn't trying to help, either. *He was exerting power,* she thinks now, startled. *He enjoyed having some power over my child.*

This wouldn't have worried her, except that it had happened so often since he moved in. She had explained and corrected and redirected, and still he took every opportunity to flex his adolescent muscles over her child. A few times is a misunderstanding; a few dozen was something else.

Her resentment wasn't helped by the fact that he'd taken over their spare room, spent thousands of (their) dollars shipping all his things from London, requested a new MacBook Pro (his had mysteriously disappeared), and had initially expressed dismay at the local high school they had taken him to tour.

All while his inheritance sat in a trust until he turned twenty-one, with no provisions for a guardian to access any of it to attend to the tasks and costs of parenting now thrust upon them.

It's the money that's the problem.

It's not as though she and Nick are struggling when it comes to money, though. They both earn a lot. Their mortgage is half paid. Nevertheless, Olivia resents spending money on things that she thinks should really have come out of Charlie's inheritance. When he turns twenty-one, he won't even need to bother with a mortgage, so drawing down on hers to buy him a fancy computer irks her considerably.

The money.

Olivia sucks in her breath. She knows she should tell the police about it. It's hardly a motive—a kidnapper isn't going to be able to access it. But Patricia had left Wolfie a considerable sum in her will. Everything else was left to Charlie, of course, but unlike Charlie's inheritance, the money left to Wolfie did stipulate a guardian could access it for basically anything related to Wolfie's well-being. Olivia wonders why Patricia hadn't thought this through better with Charlie. Or was she so delusional that she thought parenting him would be a pleasure, and the costs would be borne with a smile? Not even given a second thought?

But she pushes her indignation aside and corrects herself. Charlie is Nick's kid, too. She might be inconvenienced, but Nick is doing exactly what he should be doing: providing for his child. His ex was never that strong in the thoughtfulness department—dropping Charlie off with barely any notice when she had a big meeting to attend, or sending invoices for "Nick's half" of things she had bought him without even discussing it with Nick—but it's not like Nick is doing her a favor.

Olivia puts her head in her hands. Charlie in her kitchen is grating on her. She just needs to think. To focus. She needs to think about Wolfie, but Charlie there, making ice cream, it's like someone sitting with a stick poking into her thoughts, relentlessly. She can't think straight. She needs to sleep; she needs Charlie to be out of sight. She needs to work out the money problem, too.

Focus, focus. Olivia squeezes her eyes tightly shut, like a toddler, pretending if she can't see Charlie, he and his intrusiveness will disappear too. And even though Wolfie is crowding her mind, she pushes thoughts of him aside, methodical. *The money. Maybe the money is one problem she can solve right now.*

Her furtive dealings with her lawyer are going to look suspicious. Hell, they *are* suspicious—keeping the money left to Wolfie a secret from her husband, for a start. How is she going to explain it to Nick, let alone the police?

Not for the first time, Olivia questions her own sanity.

What was she thinking?

She supposes she could tell Nick she wanted to surprise him. Get everything set up. Organized. So then it's just a pleasant surprise. A little something to help them along, with school fees, maybe. Some family holidays.

Before Wolfie disappeared, she'd felt petulant. *What was Patricia even thinking, leaving that amount to a four-year-old?* It didn't make any sense. Even in death, was she trying to be the better person? Breezily showing off her wealth, her goodness? Why would anyone leave two hundred thousand dollars to their ex's child with another woman? Was it generosity, or something murkier?

Of course, she could say nothing. Paul hadn't lodged any of the papers. She could shrug and tell Nick that she'd just left it with her lawyer to work out the details and get back to her, and had forgotten about it. Pretend she thought it was two thousand dollars, nothing much to worry about. It wasn't that unbelievable—Nick's ex-girlfriend leaving their child two hundred thousand dollars was the unbelievable part.

For some reason Olivia finds herself clenching her jaw again. Nick would never understand it. The more she thinks about it, the more certain she is that Patricia's motives were dark. Patricia wasn't being generous. She was taunting them. That she was so successful. That she would be the one to make such a big impact on Wolfie's life. She'd looked at them so smugly when Nick had told her they couldn't afford to fly Charlie back and forth from London for visits; she'd breezily stated that she'd cover it, not to worry about it. And then had not paid one single time, and been evasive every time Nick asked if she'd pay for Charlie to come for an extra visit.

Years later, Charlie had made some comment about how the flights "weren't that much money," implying that Nick wasn't pulling his weight, and Olivia had wondered what Patricia had said to him on the topic.

Something self-serving, she imagined.

But Patricia isn't here; she can't enjoy whatever it is she was intending with the money. Olivia could easily just never tell Wolfie about where it came from, so maybe she's wrong. Maybe Patricia was just being generous. Maybe she wanted to be remembered well.

Two hundred thousand dollars.

God.

It's overwhelming. Olivia can't sort out her thoughts, let alone come to any decisions. She's left with a gnawing resentment; it's just another problem to solve. She knows it's petty, and not the real issue, but she thinks the whole thing is completely unacceptable. Particularly now that her plan of what to do about it has been upended.

"Good," she tells Charlie now, her voice forced. "But can you please leave making ice cream for another day? I need some quiet in here for a while."

13

———

FRIDAY

Thud, thud, thud.

Nick stares straight ahead, not seeing the television on the wall opposite him, not listening to the top twenty pop music blaring from speakers dotted around the gym. He's set the treadmill for forty minutes and he moves methodically. He doesn't adjust the incline or the speed. He sets and forgets and he runs, tuning out everything.

It's a forty-minute reprieve from the rest of his life.

When he finishes, he'll shower and make his way slowly home, where the days are blurring in to each other and life is shrouded in a stifling grey fog.

There are updates from police. There are more questions, more people to talk to. Olivia is shutting herself further and further away, and Nick worries about her. But he's focused on the task at hand: helping the police. To sit still and feel deeply does not seem helpful to him. He spends his time working, trying to remember additional details leading up to Wolfie's disappearance, and fielding phone calls from police.

Just once more he's visited Hannah. Just to distract himself.

Just to not think about Wolfie for one tiny sliver of his day. To try to not drown in it. Because though he is good at the tasks, when they're all done, when he's just left by himself—because Olivia is aloof and distant, and even when she's there he feels completely alone—it's unbearable, it's crushing him. The complete opposite of Olivia, he had, at the start, found something compelling about Hannah being loud, mischievous, raunchy and...available. Now, though, the whole thing strikes him as hollow and meaningless. His child is missing, and Hannah had patted him gingerly on the back, her distaste in the subject jarringly apparent. She'd been so quick to change the topic, to start taking off his clothes.

What was he thinking?

On some level, Nick knows that he started fooling around with Hannah long before he and Olivia were having any difficulties, so his petulant comparisons are not a valid excuse. But on the other hand, it is very hard to continually look at the difficult, less likeable parts of yourself. He has found a way to justify both his love for his wife and his affair with Hannah to himself, such that he can carry on with both and feel comfortable—happy, even. Sometimes, he even tells himself that he's doing Olivia a favor. That she's lost interest in him; that he's not pestering her for intimacy she doesn't desire.

Today, for the first time, though, he feels something different.

He's so long been the one in the "wrong," it takes him a while to recognize the feeling. It sits with him, a vague discomfort, something not quite right, all through the day, niggling and prickling.

Thud, thud, thud.

Usually, running helps him to tune everything out. But today his mind won't quieten. And eventually he is surprised to realize he is angry with Olivia.

Looking after Wolfie is her only job. She's been on leave for two months. She took Wolfie out of childcare, where, it seems, he would have been a whole lot safer than at home with his mother.

What was she doing while Wolfie vanished into thin air?

How on earth do you not notice your child is gone for so long that there's no trace of him?

14

"You haven't been a very caring stepmother to Charlie."

The memory of Bing's words hang in Olivia's mind as she tries to focus on Detective Rolands.

"I'm sorry?" she says.

"Things have changed a lot for your family recently. Charlie coming to live with you full-time. How has that been?"

Olivia looks out the window.

How has that been?

She thinks back to the last time she spoke to her sister. Her devastation. Bing's words as good as winding her, the air knocked out of her lungs, her metaphorical gasping to breathe. To stay alive.

It wasn't just that Bing didn't see her—her effort, her struggle with step-parenting. The hours and hours of trying. Of thinking. Of managing. Of planning and sacrificing. It was that Bing was one of only two people she confided in about step-parenting. That she had trusted her sister so much that she had honestly shared her experience and her fears and her doubts. She had trusted Bing completely. Said to her the things that she couldn't say to Nick. She had never considered for a moment that Bing was sitting in judgement—and even if she was, she would never have imagined that judgement to be so wrong. Because whatever she shared with Bing, back then, Charlie had loved her. Charlie was oblivious to her internal wrangling with the difficulties of being a stepmother. Charlie ran to her, his arms wide, his laugh gurgling all over their house.

He had certainly loved her.

She was sure of it.

How had it all gone so wrong since then?

"It's been hard," Olivia answers. She watches Rolands warily. Nick isn't with her, and she checks herself. It would be so easy just to spill everything she's thinking right now.

"He left...four years ago?" Rolands checks her notepad, glances back at Olivia, who nods.

"Just after Wolfie was born."

Things had shifted by then, definitely. She remembers the flooding relief when Nick told her Patricia's proposal. She'd been offered an amazing opportunity in London. She really wanted to take it. *It's just for a couple of years,* Patricia had urged them. *You guys will be so busy with the baby it'll fly by.*

Nick had been reluctant, obviously. He worried about Charlie missing out on that relationship with Wolfie; he wanted Charlie to be part of their family. But Olivia had been ashamed of how joyful she had felt. The older Charlie became, the less she and Nick agreed on how to parent him. Olivia valued boundaries and routine and structure. She had rules and expectations. Nick was much more laissez-faire, and gave Charlie freedoms and autonomy she wouldn't dream of giving an eleven-year-old. Charlie decided, for example, how much screen time he had on any given day. And he never ended up doing any of his chores, because Nick never insisted they were completed before gaming.

Plus, there was something unsettling about the boy. He lied, for a start. And sometimes, Olivia would catch him doing exactly what she'd asked him not to do, the look on his face not that of a rebellious or stubborn child testing the boundaries, but of someone pulling a string here and there, watching the reaction.

Calculating. That was what Olivia thought. He watched things, his face impassive, calculating what he could get away with. Stupid things. Things that didn't even matter.

She felt nervous about him being around the baby, though she couldn't form rational sentences as to why.

"How was that? Him leaving just when Wolfie came along?"

Olivia doesn't understand this new angle of questioning, but it's a relief to be honest with someone. She stopped being honest with Nick on this subject a long time ago.

"It was a reprieve, to be honest. Charlie is...not like other boys his age. He never was. I worried that he wouldn't follow instructions with the baby. That he'd have a 'good idea' that was actually dangerous or something. He often thinks that he knows best, and he gets a bit like a dog with a bone. Just pushes on with a plan, and will disregard whatever he's been asked or told. It was one less stress with a new baby."

She doesn't mention her murkier fears on this subject. That time at the playground with their friends from the country. They hadn't seen them for a year. Their daughter was three, all flying curls and bubbly laughter. And Charlie was pushing her on the swing, higher and higher. Olivia kept glancing at the girl's mother, sure she'd caution him to tone it down. And when she didn't, just as Olivia was rising from her seat to shout, "Not so high, Charlie!" the little girl had flown out of the swing, arcing through the air as though in slow motion, the crunch of her arm meeting the sawdust still making Olivia's stomach squeeze and her torso hunch over involuntarily, after all these years.

Nick had called it an accident, but Olivia had watched

Charlie's face afterward. That passive, secretive look. The coldness of it. The rote way he expressed his apologies.

The arm had broken in two places. No one was upset. They all accepted it was an accident. They tried to reassure Charlie, to ensure he didn't feel bad. They even thanked him for trying to entertain their daughter.

Olivia thought they needn't have worried. She was pretty sure Charlie didn't feel bad at all.

Cause and effect. He was just interested in the fallout.

"I see. Did Nick agree?"

"God, no," Olivia looks at Rolands uneasily. "It's an ongoing point of disagreement. It sounds so clichéd." Olivia frowns. "The evil stepmother. Glad when the stepchild is gone."

"Not at all," Rolands offers, kindly. "Parenting is hard. Step-parenting is harder. I couldn't do it."

Olivia jumps on this eagerly. It's the first piece of personal information Rolands has shared. She desperately wants to feel understood, vindicated.

I'm not a bad person.

It's just a hard gig.

"How has it been since he's been back? Has it been like you feared?"

But Olivia clams up. She feels suddenly like she's exposed too much. Nick would be livid. Charlie is just a kid, after all. And the things that she's noticed—she knows how they will sound. How *she* will sound.

Bing's words echo in her ears.

She suddenly needs to get out of there. She doesn't want Rolands asking too many questions about her family.

Lots of ghosts in those cupboards.

Things that shouldn't be exposed to the light.

15

———

Olivia holds the phone stiffly.

Her parents have it on speakerphone, and the experience always makes Olivia tense, missing child or not. Now both closer to eighty than seventy, they never remember to speak to the phone, and their voices are endlessly muffled, directed out the window or to each other. She always hangs up, realizing too late how tensely she's been sitting, her shoulders aching, her teeth on edge.

Now, they're offering help. *Should they come down? Should Olivia come up? Does she need any help?*

She wants to scream down the phone at them. She wishes she had parents who knew how to help, who were effective and useful. Her parents can't even join the dots enough to realize her staying with them in Sydney, while her child is missing in Melbourne, is the least helpful thing they could possibly offer.

They mean well, she knows that. They're doing their best, holding together their own grief and fear to try to support her. But when they ask, "Do you need any help?" she wants to shake them and shake them and scream at the sun.

She wants them to know how to help her, instinctively, without her having to ask or spell it out for them. Because right now, she herself has no idea what help she needs or how to help herself.

What do you need when your child is missing?

Your child back.

She doesn't need someone to cook meals or babysit a fifteen-year-old or rub her shoulders or even hold her.

She just wants her fucking child *back.*

And—given that they managed to lose one of their own, and they never got him back—they are the last people on earth qualified to help with that.

AFTER SHE HANGS UP, her words forced, Olivia thinks about her siblings.

Their brother, Abby, was long gone the first time that Bing attacked her.

She and Bing knew better than to ask any questions about him, and Olivia clung to Bing even more desperately in the years that followed. She—mistakenly, as it happened—thought that as the only remaining siblings, their bond was more special and more essential than ever.

As an adult, she thinks that it's probably not such an unusual dynamic. The younger sister hero-worshipping the older one. Younger siblings often seem to admire their older siblings excessively.

Until they learn better.

So she would trot around after her big sister like Bing was the only thing that mattered on the planet. Bing would wave her hands about with casual authority, commanding Olivia to do her bidding. And Olivia did it with pleasure. She wanted Bing to need her; to stay close to her; to not just disappear, as apparently it was possible for siblings to do. But sometimes she wonders if it would have been that way, anyway.

If Abby had still been with them, would she have been quite so eager and compliant? Quite so easily manipulated? Olivia thinks about that sometimes, but she'll never have an answer, because Abby wasn't with them and he wasn't coming back.

But even that first time that Olivia said no to Bing, and the fallout felt nuclear, things didn't change. Olivia would spend years trying to understand the dynamic between them and blaming herself every time things went wrong. And that first time—it was a minor thing. So minor Olivia can't even remember it now. Was it Bing asking to borrow her favorite jeans, or ride her bike somewhere? And good little Olivia, obedient little Olivia, desperate-for-her-sibling's-love Olivia—testing her thirteen-year-old wings and perhaps for the first time feeling taken advantage of by her sister—casually said "no."

The barrage of abuse (*after all the things I do for you—selfish little brat—think your things are too good to share with me—no one likes you anyway—I heard Mum telling Dad what a bore you are*) was delivered with such violent rage that Olivia fled to her wardrobe floor and lay there in the fetal position for hours. Her mother found her there, shuddering, so devastated and confused by the attack that she couldn't even speak of it. It wasn't even the words so much, but the delivery—the flying spit, the savage set of her mouth, the unadulterated hatred in Bing's eyes. Olivia saw her as a wild dog, killing for pleasure. Intent on destruction, at any cost.

Bing didn't speak to her for four days, by which time Olivia was convinced that she had indeed done something horribly wrong. She was so confused; it was so nonsensical that when Bing asked her for the next favor, she scrambled to oblige.

This cycle repeated throughout the next two decades—when Olivia asserted a boundary or disagreed with her sister, she was savaged so violently that she sobbed for days—until the comment about Charlie just before Wolfie was born. Olivia had just asserted that Bing would need to wait for Olivia to okay a visit to the hospital to meet him—she was anxious about how the birth would go, and found the idea of visitors immediately afterwards overwhelming.

"I'll call you as soon as I'm ready for visitors," Olivia had said, herself understanding the comment to be an invitation, extending something precious to someone special. But she could see Bing's face tightening, the jeering edge to her jaw that Olivia had come to know so well. And though Olivia could see that Bing was struggling with something upon hearing this news, she could not for the life of her work out how Bing could interpret her wanting a few hours to recover—after pushing a *live human being out of her vagina*—as a slight or a dismissal or something to take personally and be affronted by.

She felt the familiar churning in her stomach. Bing's anger was never terribly rational, but always terribly painful.

"I'm worried about how you'll find mothering," she'd said, so casually it still takes Olivia's breath away. Her features had been rearranged into something like concern, but Olivia could read the gloating underneath. The satisfaction of finding something to hurt Olivia with.

For a moment, Olivia tried not to rise, not to bite—to just ignore the comment completely. But she couldn't help herself. She did what Bing expected her to do: she asked her why.

"You just don't seem to be a very nurturing person." And then, after a pause: "You haven't been a very caring stepmother to Charlie."

And finally, *finally,* Olivia had come to see the pattern: Bing could not tolerate her little sister disagreeing with her or asserting a boundary. It made no sense—Bing seemed to be able to navigate all her other relationships outside of her family of origin with ease, with professional accolades, endless invitations to interesting people's parties, and friends who would rave about how supportive she'd been through a difficult period in their lives. Yet she was so undeniably violent and irrational every time that Olivia didn't acquiesce to her, that Olivia had started to distance herself from Bing. She missed her sister, but she was no longer tiptoeing around trying to avoid the next emotional beating. For most of Wolfie's short little life, she had congratulated herself on this decision. It was hard, but for her own good. Bing was not to be trusted with her heart. And because her attacks were so nonsensical—*juvenile,* even—Olivia felt powerless to resolve the issue. Every time she had tried, Bing recounted a perspective so far from Olivia's that they didn't seem to be talking about the same event. These conversations always ended with Bing crying about how badly she was hurt, painting Olivia as the aggressor, and playing the victim.

Disengaging was a relief.

It wasn't enough, though.

Distancing was not the same as asserting herself.

It was funny, because she didn't think of herself as a vengeful person. Not usually. And she'd felt so grown up, so proud, to cut off contact and just *stop.* Stop trying to explain to Bing, stop trying to get her to understand, stop being blindsided by her rage and her tantrums and her rigid adherence to her own interpretations of the world.

She walked away, and she felt just fine.

For a while.

16

———

Nick is up early.

He pauses at the door of his bedroom, his eyes resting on Olivia. She's sleeping, but not deeply. Her breath is shallow.

Once, this would have inspired tenderness. He might have made her a cup of tea, or even just watched her for a while, looking forward to her waking, being present with him again. Today, though, it fills him with a sense of urgency.

He wants to be gone before she wakes.

In the kitchen, Charlie offers him a coffee. He smiles at his son. He's grown tall, embodying that awkward teenage lankiness. *He's such a thoughtful kid*, Nick thinks. He knows the coffee will be over frothed and not hot enough, but he accepts the offer gratefully anyway. He loves how helpful Charlie is being around the house. He's really making an effort and Nick is proud of him.

"What are you up to today?" he asks as Charlie busies himself at the coffee machine. Nick shoves a slice of bread in the toaster, wondering if he can take both in the car. He's relieved to just have a normal conversation. He's desperate about Wolfie, too. But he just can't handle the constant misery, the focus on it. He wants to *do* things. Be helpful. Olivia's approach—every waking moment concentrating on the misery —makes him breathless, panicked. The police are doing their work. There's been a sighting, in Chadstone. The police doubt its validity, but at least it means the community is looking. Everyone is looking for Wolfie. He just wants to let the professionals do what needs to be done. He knows they will find him.

His mind shies away from any other option. Unlike Olivia, he can't let himself imagine. *Where is Wolfie? Who is with him? What are they doing to him? Is he...hurt?*

Olivia sobs and screams when she lets herself imagine. Nick tries to help her shut these thoughts out, but she seems to think she is doing a disservice to Wolfie if she doesn't consider and fully feel the pain of every possible scenario. It's a type of insanity he cannot comprehend. And so he works, he returns phone calls, he keeps his chin up and tells himself it's for Charlie that he's holding everything together—but that is not true. He cannot reckon with the darkness that comes with those questions. On some very deep level, he knows that way lies madness, a grief so sharp he will never come back from it. There are possibilities his mind cannot tolerate considering. They will break him, and he will never put himself back together.

Charlie hands him his coffee.

"I might go to the skate park," he says, his eyes not quite meeting Nick's. "It's a nice day to get out."

"Good idea," Nick encourages. For the briefest of moments, he wonders about that evasiveness, but decides Charlie might feel guilty about going out and enjoying himself, under the circumstances. It doesn't occur to him to ask, or acknowledge it; that a greater intimacy might lie that way. "Wear sunscreen," he says, instead, grabbing his toast and heading for the door. He doesn't stop to butter it. He's desperate to go before Olivia wakes and passes judgement on his participation in such domestic normalcy.

He just needs to get out of this house.

He just needs to not be suffocating.

NICK NEEDN'T HAVE WORRIED—WHEN Olivia stirs, she makes no move to get out of bed. Instead, she lies there wondering where it all went so wrong.

It was only a couple of short years ago that everything had been fine. Back then, the differences in their parenting styles were barely noticeable. Olivia's concerns those last few years before Charlie left for London had faded away. But it was about then, she thinks now, that things started to get harder. The divergence in their parenting styles was certainly starting to grate on her after Wolfie's second birthday.

There was the camping trip, for a start. And not long after that, scrabbling through some papers, trying to find the last payment for their ambulance cover after childcare forms asked for the number (*God, have we renewed it?* she had worried. *I haven't seen it for years*) Olivia found payments going to Charlie. He was thirteen years old, and Nick was sending him one hundred dollars a week.

When she confronted him, he seemed perplexed.

"London's expensive. He needs some pocket money," he'd said. And dismissed her concerns that he should have discussed it with her first; and that it was an awful lot of pocket money for a thirteen-year-old. When the argument escalated, he'd said—not for the first time—"He's my son. I get to decide." Olivia—also not for the first time—felt sucker punched.

She still remembers how that felt.

"I got to share the drop-offs and pick-ups for ten years, I got to take time off work to take him the doctor when he was sick, I got to help with the homework, pay for half of everything, but *you* get to make the decisions?" she'd asked, incredulous.

"You don't do those things anymore," Nick had said, and walked out the door.

Thinking about it now, Olivia feels foolish. She and Nick didn't talk about anything when it came to how they wanted to parent. She flew into it, eyes wide shut, bolstered by love. Even though she had evidence right in front of her eyes about how parenting with Nick might go.

For some reason, she thought it would be different with Wolfie.

With *her*.

Nick and Patricia had separated when Charlie was barely born. She reasoned that Nick felt guilty, and overcompensated. Didn't seek any information or parenting support. Just winged it without someone like her to help him. God, when she first met him, he didn't even put Charlie to bed. Just let him sit up watching TV until he fell asleep on the couch.

The fights with Charlie when she instigated a bedtime routine were just the start of all the time and effort and energy she'd devoted to being a good stepparent.

But by the end of Wolfie's third year, she knew that Nick's ideas about parenting were just not the same as hers.

And sometimes, as much as she doubts her own capacity, she thinks Wolfie would be much better off if Nick just fucked right off out of the picture altogether.

CHARLIE PLACES the newspaper on the table carefully.

He's longing to cut the article out—he's started a collection of them, and the idea of one being missing unsettles him. But he can cut it out later, he tells himself.

When Olivia comes in to the kitchen a few minutes later, it's the first thing she sees.

The headline stops her in her tracks. One arm is reaching up to brush a stray hair from her face, and it stops there, a comical pose that would be more in place in a children's cartoon than in the kitchen of a woman who has lost her son.

MISSING BOY'S WARRING PARENTS

The picture of Wolfie is not the one they supplied to police, his blond curls shining, his big blue eyes wide with laughter. That picture makes Olivia's heart ache every time she looks at it.

How larger than life he seems.

How joyful.

How innocent.

This picture is grainier. Wolfie is frowning at something. Olivia knows it is his favorite truck puzzle. He has nearly completed it by himself for the first time. Olivia took the photo on her phone. Moments later, she took another, his face triumphant. She remembers that day, like she remembers all his days, in vivid detail.

Long days, fast years.

He had run to her, cackling with glee, and she'd lifted a hand for a high five, but he'd crashed into her arms for a cuddle instead, the puzzle already forgotten in the delight he found in the attention of his mother.

But without context, Wolfie looks...wrong. Like he is a sad child, left alone, frowning down to the side like he has worries far bigger than a four-year-old should ever have to carry. Like he has to stare at the floor, alone. It shifts the narrative somehow, so subtly that it will take Olivia hours to work out why it enrages and unsettles her, even more than the headline.

Now, though, she moves slowly to the table and sits heavily in the nearest chair. She unfolds the paper slowly and starts reading, her chest tight.

New information in the case of missing four-year-old Wolfie Hitchens suggests all was not well between his parents, Olivia Shorten and Nick Hitchens, sparking new questions about his whereabouts.

An anonymous source claims that Wolfie's mother, Olivia, has been seen leaving the offices of prominent divorce lawyer Paul O'Brien, in the city's wealthy Eastern suburbs. O'Brien has declined to comment. Meanwhile, the hunt for Wolfie across the nation is now entering its second week.

Sixth day, Olivia thinks to herself, automatically.

It's been six days, and Olivia feels every moment of every one of them as needles scratching across the surface of her, cutting fine lines into her skin. She recoils at even the thought of a second week. Two weeks without Wolfie is not possible to fathom.

It wasn't unreasonable, she supposes. Paul's offices are one of many in the building, but someone might have recognized her from the press conference. She's more interested in the photo. How did this trashy newspaper get that photo? She probably posted it to Facebook, sure. But her privacy settings are as private as is possible; only her close friends and family would have access to it. And it was taken months ago. There must have been hundreds of photos posted since then.

Even if someone somehow got access to her profile, and scrolled back and back, looking for something (what? Dirt, of some kind?), why would they choose that one? Why show Wolfie looking unhappy, appearing unloved?

She checks her email. Paul would never call her; he's too discreet. As expected, there's a message from him: *call me when you can.* But she doesn't have the wherewithal just yet. She tells herself it's trash journalism—no one reads that paper anyway. But she imagines she can feel the shift in the Australian air, a tiny movement carried on the dust and the heat through the scorching outback, all the way through the sprawling suburbs with their neat green lawns to her front door. A slight hum or crackle. Something troubling and visceral.

People love a good villain.

Frantic parents trying to find their beautiful boy are different from feuding parents going through an ugly divorce.

The truth need not even come into the picture.

17

———

Saturday

Nick taps his foot impatiently.

He's been back from walking the streets for hours, and Olivia is not at home. She hasn't told him where she would be. Usually this would be inconsequential, but today it irks Nick. Their child is missing—he feels more entitled than usual to a minute-by-minute account of her whereabouts.

Especially given the newspaper article lying on their kitchen table.

He doesn't notice the irony of this sentiment, given he had wanted to leave the house before she was awake, not to mention his visits to Hannah—but even if he did think about these things, he would justify to himself that things were different now.

Bad press doesn't just feel bad. He knows instinctively that it will be unhelpful for finding Wolfie.

Something churns in his stomach. It's partly anxiety *—surely he would notice if his wife was thinking about leaving him?* —but it's partly just the unsettling sense of the world not turning in the way that it should.

He's made mistakes, sure. He hasn't really listened or helped Olivia with her worries about Wolfie—and now, with him missing, he can see how starkly they sit alongside her own history. A missing boy. With some behavioral problems. How did he not put two and two together? He had thought Olivia was making too much of it. He'd let her fears slide off him, barely even registering them, if he was honest. He just really expected that life would tick along and problems would come and go and it was all just part of the ebb and flow of things.

He hadn't really considered that he would need to sit down and focus on anything with his whole mind and his whole heart. And he certainly didn't notice that sometimes that "ebb and flow" of things only flowed because someone else was solving problems or taking action to keep things moving in the right direction.

Now, though, he can see how alone Olivia might have felt. *And maybe she was being a bit irrational—a bit melodramatic even* —and here he winces at the word that he's allowed himself to use every now and then when he thinks about Olivia's priorities and predilections—*but didn't she have good reason to be?*

He tries to quell his feelings of panic—that he is too late, too blind, that he hasn't noticed how unhappy Olivia is or isn't, that perhaps he has become too complacent, too selfish—by scrabbling around in his memories for something more positive to hold on to. Endlessly the optimist, even in his state of distress, his impulses are simplistic. He is soothed by just one memory, and stops searching for others: just last week, having dinner, Olivia had turned to him, her eyes brighter than they'd been for months. She'd leaned over the dinner table to kiss him, really kiss him, and he'd felt his heart flutter like it always did when he felt loved by Olivia.

She wouldn't have kissed someone she no longer loved, would she?

Her eyes held promises of more kisses, of tender touches, of dinner parties and shared successes. Of children and family and growing old together.

Of a future that held possibilities beyond measure.

He continues to sit, foot tapping. He doesn't notice Charlie come into the room, and he doesn't notice him pick up the offending paper and leave again. His thoughts are turned so far inward, making bargains and promises and deals with himself.

He'll end things with Hannah.

He'll be more helpful with Wolfie.

He'll listen to Olivia's worries more.

He'll be better, *dammit.*

If Olivia will stay with him, and Wolfie is returned to him, he will be so much, so much better.

AS HE WAITS, Nick's thoughts shift uncomfortably around his last conversation with Detective Rolands. *Was it yesterday? The day before?*

The days are all blurring into each other. Nick's tight focus on attending to things in a linear manner is starting to fray around the edges. He no longer does any work from home. The notion of keeping himself busy till his son is returned to him is laughable, now. He does not do much of anything but walk the streets and stare blankly at walls.

"Tell me a bit about Charlie and Patricia."

He'd been evasive, he knows. False cheer. The memory makes him cringe a little.

"Charlie's great!" he'd said. "He's so mature. He's really coped so well considering everything he's lost. And he's trying to help out at the moment, with everything so...hard."

"Why did you and Patricia separate?"

Nick had paused for a long moment. "Why is that relevant?" he'd said.

"I'm just trying to get a picture of the family. I don't know what might be relevant, yet," Rolands had replied. She sounded so reasonable, so patient. And Nick didn't want to come across as difficult. But he had trouble managing his irritation.

He didn't want to talk about Patricia.

"Who knows," he'd said, short, almost snappish. "Turns out I wasn't what she wanted. She didn't care to elaborate. And I didn't press for a blow-by-blow of why I wasn't good enough, funnily enough."

There was silence for a moment down the line, and Nick regretted his tone.

It also wasn't entirely true, but he didn't want to think about that, and he certainly didn't want to share it with the detective who was supposed to be out looking for his child.

Rolands didn't press for further details. "How are things between you and Olivia?" she'd asked.

But Nick didn't really want to talk about that, either.

Instead, his mind drifted to better days. His heart still tumbled to his abdomen every time he remembered the day he met Olivia.

She was beautiful, sure—but it wasn't like he hadn't been with beautiful women before.

That night, she was wearing an understated green dress, small pearls at her ears; and she had tried to slap enthusiasm on her pale, perfect face when he'd approached her. It struck him as both polite, and unnecessarily tedious. She was expecting him to bore her. He imagined she'd been approached by many men, at many parties. The look on her face suggested she would humor him for five minutes, ten if he was lucky— then she'd make an excuse and slip away.

He'd wondered why you'd bother coming to a party if you didn't really want to talk to anyone, but then he'd seen the way her face changed when Marjorie from Accounting walked past; the unadulterated joy. She had looked, for a moment, childlike in her eagerness, and Nick had wanted to make her face light up like that. He'd accosted Marjorie, drew her into conversation, asked her about her sick kid and how his recovery was going. It wasn't artifice—Nick was well-loved around the office. He remembered the details of people's lives. He always asked about them.

"What about you, Olivia?" he'd continued, after Marjorie had given him a detailed and hilarious account of the most recent hospital stay. Her son suffered from chronic asthma, and was hospitalized at least once a year. Marjorie was warm and gregarious; she made friends everywhere, and could turn even a hospital stay into a good story. Sometimes, Nick wondered if she felt she couldn't talk about the pain or the fear of it, or if she simply didn't want to. Everyone loved Marjorie; the role of entertainer looked like it could be a burden, sometimes, though.

"I haven't seen you in the office before. How long have you been with us?"

"Just a couple of weeks," Olivia had replied, but she'd turned back to Marjorie, concern in her eyes. "That must have been scary for you, though, Marj," she'd said. "Was anyone with you? Do you have enough support?" And Marjorie had faltered, just for a moment, and Olivia had caught it with ease: "It might not be the best time to talk about it. But let's have a cuppa tomorrow, okay?"

It summed up everything Nick had come to know and love about his wife—her kindness, her perceptiveness, her willingness to help. She was hard to get to know, but once he was allowed in, he couldn't believe it was actually possible to love someone so much. He kept expecting some flaw to show itself, but as the months, then years, went by, she seemed to become more and more perfect.

Until now.

"Nick?" Detective Rolands prompted him, and he wondered

how long he had been silent. How that silence could be interpreted.

He tried to bring his mind back to the question, but it stubbornly jumped instead to Patricia. Why she left him.

He wished Rolands hadn't asked those questions.

Nick has successfully not thought about the answers for years and years and years.

18

———

Saturday

"Is it true?"

Rolands is restrained, but Olivia thinks she hears an edge to her voice.

So many people wanting to talk to her.

It was easier than she would have thought to ignore them all. Except this one.

She's walking home, and she lets her pace slow to a dawdle. She's not really in a hurry to see Nick, anyway. Or the journalists who have set up camp on their street outside their house.

She wonders how much information the police are allowed access to in a kidnapping investigation. She supposes their powers extend a long way.

"He's not a divorce lawyer," she hedges down the phone. "He's an all-sorts-of-things lawyer."

Thinking about lying feels different to actually forming the words and having them come out of her mouth.

She presses on, though. "Nick's ex left Wolfie some money in her will. I'd kind of forgotten about it. Then I just thought, money can motivate people, can't it? I just wanted Paul to sort that out. See if there was anything that might be useful for you. For the investigation."

"How much money?" Rolands asks.

"A few thousand, I think. Paul is following it up." Olivia swallows. "It's weird, right? Patricia leaving money to her ex's child with someone else?"

Rolands make a noise that Olivia can't interpret. She waits.

"Are you and Nick in trouble?" she asks next.

Olivia hesitates. "I don't think so," she ventures. "Things have been hard. With Wolfie. Before. Parenting is hard, you know." She repeats Rolands' words back to her carefully. *Calculatedly,* she thinks, and pauses abruptly.

If it was Charlie saying this, what would she think?

Then she goes on: "It's hard now, of course. We're not coping...in the same way. I can't do anything else, think of anything else. It's consuming me. Nick...he just carries on. That's how he copes, how he protects himself. I know it's not fair, but I can't bear it. It looks, from the outside, like he hasn't even noticed Wolfie's gone."

<hr>

AFTER SHE HANGS UP, Olivia meanders past the playground where she usually takes Wolfie when she needs to get out of the house. It's deserted—parents are keeping their children at home under tight wraps.

Doing a better job than she had done at keeping them safe. Or trying to.

She hesitates, then goes on and sits on the swing, lets it gently move. One hinge squeaks on the forward movement, a grating noise that seems fitting to Olivia. She lets her mind wander.

What started all this? Was it the camping trip?

Wolfie was two and a half years old. And Charlie was coming from London to visit.

Now, Olivia tries to remember. Charlie must have visited before then. She was sure they hadn't gone for two-and-a-half years without seeing him. Nick would never have allowed it. But the camping trip is all she remembers when she thinks about Charlie's visits.

Nick had booked a campsite out in the country. He was as excited as a little boy: his whole family all together, going fishing, doing bushwalks. He planned menus and bought equipment and bounced around in anticipation for a full month before Charlie arrived.

Even Olivia was looking forward to it. *Surely Charlie wasn't as difficult as she remembered?* Still glowing in the joys of motherhood—Wolfie's anxiety hadn't arrived yet—she couldn't imagine that anything could be that hard. Perhaps she hadn't tried hard enough.

Perhaps she hadn't shown him enough love.

Bing's words come back to her at that moment, though, and she digs her toes into the sawdust. The swing screeches to a halt. The light seems to dim a little, and Olivia shivers. When she thinks of Bing, it's like a perpetual cloud materializes and blots out the sun.

It wasn't always like this; at one time, Bing had *been* the sun, the light and warmth that Olivia had orbited like a hapless moth. Now, though, she turns her mind away from all that dark.

Not that the camping trip is much of an improvement.

When the time finally arrived, Olivia had baked slices and packed toys and made all sorts of resolutions in her head about how much effort and love she would inject into her relationship with Charlie.

He was just a kid, after all.

She was the adult in this relationship.

What could possibly go wrong?

Slowly Olivia starts swinging again, tiny small movements. The hinge grates and screeches.

She still wonders if she imagined it. She still has moments of doubt. She knows she is too controlling. But who gets to draw the line over which "good enough" parenting occurs and the child thrives? What is good enough to someone else is not good enough for Olivia. She worries and frets over so many things.

Someone once told her that you only need to be attuned to your child thirty percent of the time to reach that magic line. *Thirty percent.* She doesn't believe this statistic, and means to look it up, but never does; in itself a strange anomaly, for someone who strives so resolutely toward perfection. Perhaps its confirmation would have soothed her.

Perhaps she would have done things differently.

But she doesn't look it up, and she frets when Nick sips his coffee and reads his paper and doesn't respond to Wolfie's bids for his attention. It feels like something physical inside her: a rising up of a scratchy lump from her abdomen, pushing upwards, relentless. She can't quell her agitation; she has to let it out.

Don't make it shit, she thinks: and then she goes ahead and makes it shit, with snarky comments, rigid posture, heavy sighs. The relief of it like taking her feet off the pedals and roaring downhill, too fast, on a bicycle. Knowing you're going to crash and burn but being soothed by that brief window of surrender anyway.

She always goes to Wolfie.

Nick never even notices, unless she snaps.

Which she does sometimes.

Nick remembers it differently. He remembers Olivia rigid and inflexible, pandering to Wolfie's every holler.

He remembers her ruining his holiday, his special time with Charlie, his first long visit since he moved overseas.

He remembers for the first time not loving Olivia quite so much anymore.

Now, though, Nick's sitting at the kitchen table. He's still there when Olivia comes home.

"Where have you been?" he asks, his voice hard.

"Walking," she replies. Irked by his belief that he has something to be angry about.

"What's with the lawyer?"

Olivia glances at Charlie, who is loitering at the fridge. Was that the hint of a smile, before he turned away? He takes a seat on the lounge, and Olivia hates that he doesn't take his cue to leave them to a private conversation.

Is that unreasonable? she wonders. *Do teenagers pick up on social cues?*

"Would you mind giving us some privacy, Charlie?" she says pointedly, and waits while he shuffles down the hall. Nick watches her the whole time, his posture stiff.

Olivia turns back to him, working to keep her face neutral. "Patricia left him a couple thousand dollars in her will. I had forgotten about it. But I suddenly thought maybe it was important. I don't know. It's weird, right?" She repeats the line she used with Rolands earlier. There's a lot of other pieces of that information Nick could focus on. She wants him to focus on the strangeness of Patricia's last wishes.

"What?" Nick looks confused. This was not the way he expected this conversation to go. "How did you even know about it?" he adds, a moment later, struggling to catch up. He shakes his head slightly, as though he might shake away the puzzling nature of it, the sticky threads catching in his mind.

"A letter came ages ago from her solicitor. I just sent it to Paul to deal with. I found it really strange. I mean there's no provisions to help us to support Charlie, but Wolfie gets something? It made me feel uncomfortable. So I sent it off for Paul to work out. And then, with everything else going on, I guess I forgot about it. But money..." Olivia lets her voice trail off. She leaves it to Nick to join the dots.

Glancing at him, she thinks he does indeed look confused. And...guilty? Sheepish? Something moves across his face, but it is gone before she can put her finger on it. She'll replay that look later, try to figure it out. Maybe he knew Patricia was leaving Wolfie something. But he doesn't correct her on the amount, if that's the case.

"What did Paul say?" he asks.

"Nothing," Olivia says. "I didn't have an appointment. I just stuck my head in the door and asked him to chase it up and let me know what happens. I should have emailed. But I needed a walk. It was something to do."

She lets the sentiment hang there, suspended. A tiny droplet of all the time that surrounds her, that she has to fill in before Wolfie comes back to her. Before she can breathe in his smell and hold him tight.

Before she can acknowledge his fingers or say good night twenty times.

Whatever he needs.

She will do it all.

Nick has no reason to not believe her, and she moves mechanically around the kitchen. She's not hungry, but food preparation gives her hands and mind something to focus on. She takes some chicken out of the freezer and runs some hot water in the sink. She knows it will take too long to defrost, and she hates defrosting in the microwave. But hell, she can't think beyond a stir-fry. Coming up with that is as much problem-solving as her mind can take right now.

Nick is silent, and as she chops and sautés, the edges of her mind pick at her relationship with Charlie.

When she was younger, she would never have imagined it was difficult to love a kid. Their joyfulness, the way they threw their love around, recklessly, exuberantly; just being near kids made her smile. The thought of any child, anywhere, not getting the love it deserved from the adults around it filled her heart with such heaviness and despair that she couldn't think about it. Of all the charities she donated to, none were to orphanages or places to support abused or neglected children, despite the fact that this was the cause in which she most passionately believed. But it was too painful for her to even look at their websites: her mind shied away from them instinctively, slippery and unfocused.

Untethered.

Children not getting the love they deserved untethered her.

It was tied up in the pain that surrounded Abby, even though Abby was loved.

He was.

Just not enough.

And here she was, mother of two. Struggling to manage her feelings.

Struggling to love.

How naïve she had been, she thinks to herself. To think that simply being near a child was enough to ensure that you loved them. That all children were loveable, just by the fact of their age.

That all children were good and deserving.

That none of them should be hurt, or lonely, or held down in anger.

That none of them should be cut free.

19

Saturday

At 10 p.m. on the dot, Ray's phone rings, and he smiles.

His smile fades as his partner starts talking, though.

"Slow down, slow down," he interrupts, struggling to make sense of what is being said to him.

"When are you coming home?" is all that he can understand.

"You know that," Ray says, his voice soothing. "It's on the calendar. It's just three more days. What's wrong? What's going on?"

It's always been this way: Ray, being the anchor, holding things together. Which was odd, when you thought about it, because Ray was also the one that had served time, had bounced in and out of juvenile detention, angry and on edge. It was probably this relationship that saved him, pulled him out of something dark, gave him something meaningful to contribute. Looking after someone else somehow spilled over into looking after himself.

His mind drifts back to Mandy. Mandy had wanted to wade into that day: his mum. The car ride out of Melbourne. How

Ray got here, to this place, inside lockup, but also inside his own head, where he was also locked up, and it was bleak and lonely and painful in both places.

He could never go there with Mandy. What she knew, she had gleaned from his case file, and police reports. His mother's murder. What he'd seen. Unspeakable things.

He'd been so little. He can't believe he survived. He can't even think about it. But somehow, he could go there in love. He could talk about it, to just this one person.

Nobody else.

I just don't know what to do with this, is all he hears now. For the first time, he wishes they had a Mandy in their lives again, because he doesn't know what to do with it either. For so long, it's just been the two of them—no family. No support. No intrusion. They have no roadmap to follow when police come knocking on your door. Police have never had something to give, only something to take. So it's hard not to think that only grief will come of this.

But the police just asked a few questions, and left again. *That was the end of it, right?* There was no indication that they'd be back, that they needed anything else.

Now, though, he makes soothing noises. He encourages apathy—*just wait till I get home. Don't do anything. We'll work it out together.*

And he hopes to God no more police go knocking on their door.

20

Four Months Earlier

Wolfie is crouched on the loungeroom floor, his mouth puckered in concentration.

Olivia watches him carefully line up his matchbox cars.

He makes a perfect line, in a perfect rainbow.

The fire engine he keeps in his hand, frowning.

It's three o'clock in the afternoon, and Olivia has a large glass of chardonnay in hand. She called in sick to work, unable to gather enough strength and headspace to leave Wolfie at childcare. His distress is so enormous, so palpable, so consuming, that lying on the couch with a glass of wine seems like a sensible alternative.

The educators talk to her in hushed voices. *Have there been any changes at home? Is there something Wolfie is worried about?*

Olivia doesn't have answers to these questions. What are the changes that you can quantify to explain such nervousness? Wolfie, once joyful, now keeps to himself, watching the other children but refusing to join in any activities with them.

"He's become very quiet," the educators tell her, curious, worried.

There is nothing at home that Olivia would consider warrants such a change. Nick and her are drifting apart, but it's a quiet drift. There are no arguments. Nick stays back later and later at the office; Olivia rushes to pick Wolfie up, shore him up with love and kisses, spend quiet time with him to help him regulate after the stress he's been displaying at pickup. All day, by all accounts.

And then, exhausted, she snaps at him and feels herself defined by sharp edges and harsh lines—all the things she is rushing home early to protect him from. Only to find them in herself.

Kiss, kiss, pinch a little.

This erosion of her sanity is unexpected. She finds herself wishing for bygone eras, where she could stay at home, consumed only by her child, without the stress and pressures of work deadlines and creative briefs she can no longer focus on. She thinks about her grandmother in a different light. Because no one warned her how hard it would be, this adulting business. How anyone managed to parent, and work, and run a house, and maintain a marriage. *Did other people find it easier? Did anyone else feel like they might crack under all the pressure?*

She resents Nick's ability to shut it all out. *Was he always like this?* she wonders, now. She remembers Nick being attentive, attuned, thoughtful. *When did it change? Was it only since Wolfie was born? Is it only parenting that divides them?*

"He'll grow out of it," he says, whenever she tries to talk to him about it. And goes back to his laptop.

While Olivia worries that they are failing him somehow.

Now, she drinks too much chardonnay. She scrolls through her Facebook feed. She hates that Nick isn't trying harder, while she falls short of all the bars she sets, herself.

"How's step-parenting?" Bing texts, and Olivia jerks upright, and spills chardonnay all over her shirt. And then: "I'm thinking of giving it a go myself."

21

———————

"DON'T BE AN IDIOT."

Johnny shakes his head, but Ray can't read his expression. Is Johnny angry with him?

"I was just trying to get us some bloody dinner."

"I told you how to get us the bloody dinner. And it doesn't involve stealing shit and bringing the cops down on our heads."

"Yeah? Well maybe I'm sick of begging from dawn till dusk for a few measly dollars. Maybe I just wanted to eat till I'm full for a change." He digs into his stolen stash ferociously. It's not the first time he's taken things, but it's easily the most he's taken, and he had been feeling good until he'd showed Johnny.

Proud.

Jesus.

For a few minutes he gorges on chocolate. One bar, two, three. Finally, he throws one over to where Johnny sits, nestled in boxes and blankets. It's cold, and they usually take turns begging.

He watches Johnny from lowered eyes.

For a minute he thinks Johnny isn't going to take the chocolate bar. He sits stiffly in the dark, then he reaches out slowly and takes it, unwraps it methodically. Their eyes meet, and Johnny doesn't look away, from the first bite until the last.

"Thank you," he says, eventually. "But please don't bring that shit back here again."

22

———

SUNDAY

"Do you think you'll have another baby?"

Nick is startled out of his reverie.

Charlie is offering him a coffee, as has become his habit these last few days. Nick supposes he's trying in his own small way to be helpful, when he must see that Olivia and Nick are completely falling apart.

Even to Nick, who's so resolutely positive and optimistic and committed to seeing the best in people, it's an oddly timed question. It feels almost like Charlie is offering up a solution: *well this one's missing, how about we just get another?*

They had talked about it, Olivia and him. It seems ridiculous now. It wasn't long after Charlie's second visit—Nick had been so high on family love juices he would have had ten more, if Olivia had agreed to it. But she'd been oddly resistant.

"What makes you think that's a good idea?" she'd said, the movement of her coffee cup abruptly stopping halfway to her lips at the proposition, so much so that the hot liquid slopped over the lip, dripping onto Olivia's skirt. She hadn't flinched, her eyes intent on Nick, watchful.

Wolfie had been about to celebrate his third birthday, and Patricia's stint in London was—for the second time, perhaps really this time—drawing to a close. The idea of pulling his family in closer and tighter and *more* was like a physical need.

He had wanted a tribe.

"Well, it's nice to have them close together, don't you think? Even if we started trying now, Wolfie would likely be four before a little brother or sister came along. Charlie will be home soon, and he's old enough to help out. I'd love to have three," Nick had told her.

Olivia had just sipped her coffee thoughtfully for a while.

"I'll think about it," she'd told Nick, but he could see in her furrowed brow and the hard, thin set of her mouth that she'd already thought about it, and she wasn't enthused. And though he'd raised it again intermittently over the next year, she was always evasive. *She wasn't sure; things were hard with Wolfie right now; could she think about it?*

Eventually he'd just let it go: resigned himself to just the two.

Was he angry about this? Disappointed? Resentful? Nick realizes with a start that he doesn't really know.

Now, Charlie's question feels painful to Nick. He can't quite put his finger on it. It might have been that what Olivia had wanted had won out over what he had wanted; or it might have been a curious and misplaced sense that the universe would have shifted had they had three: some kind of magical thinking. Wolfie would not have been on the trampoline by himself because he would have had a baby to watch over or play with. It might have even been the first experience of discomfort with Charlie—that he really wished he hadn't asked that question at this moment in time; that he couldn't fathom his motives or empathize with his clumsy attempt at conversation.

Usually, Nick wouldn't delve too deeply into his discomfit. None of these explanations would strike him as reasonable; all would thus usually be dismissed. Ever since Patricia left him, he's latched on to being the even-handed one: calm. Rational. Supportive. Giving. So when more difficult feelings start to well up, his impulse is to squash them right back down again. Sadness—resentment, even—that his desire for another child was thwarted, or that his eldest son said something insensitive at a difficult time, would normally not seem reasonable to Nick. He thinks his relationships hinge on being accommodating. Not demanding too many things. Not expecting perfection from people. Accepting that they are probably doing their best.

Somehow, through this process, he's managed to deny to himself that he's entitled to feelings, too. Partly it's protective; Patricia had taken to his sense of himself as someone worthy of love like kids to a piñata. It wasn't just being left, being rejected —Patricia had gone much further than that. It still takes his breath away. His mind has shied away from the truth of it for fifteen years.

So partly his sliding mind and relentless reasonableness is helping him to cope. To not feel the pain of it when someone he loves does wrong by him. To not leave even the smallest skerrick of room for harder questions, like *am I worthy?* Or *am I loved?*

Now, though, Nick is startled by the thought that perhaps it's also partly laziness.

It's hard to confront painful things.

It's a luxury to avoid them. A luxury that is right now being poked full of painful, sharp little holes.

"I don't think so," he says to Charlie now, taking the coffee from him, his thoughts and body sluggish, uncooperative. He sits heavily at the kitchen table. It's been seven days: he can no longer carry on with practical tasks and wait for the police to find and return his child. Somehow, in this moment, with that question, all the things he tries not to think about are crowding his brain and they won't be shoved aside. His pushing down,

pushing away is failing him. He can't keep his thoughts positive
—his resolute refusal to think about worst-case scenarios can't
be sustained anymore.

Minutes tick by. Nick sits at the table and stares into space.
He forgets about Charlie, he forgets about Hannah, he even
forgets about Olivia.

He just wants his son back.

IN THEIR BEDROOM—AND it might as well be on another
continent, she feels so distant to Nick—Olivia has stopped
getting out of bed.

She lies in an unwashed T-shirt, her mobile phone clutched
to her chest.

To an outsider, it would look like she is waiting for a call
from the police. The call that they have found Wolfie. That he
is fine; that he is coming home.

But that's not why she clutches the phone to her chest.

She's thinking about making a phone call. She wants to.
She doesn't want to.

As she swings wildly between calling and not calling, she
squeezes the phone to her then holds it away from her. She will
hold it close and not call. She will allow herself to open it, go to
her contacts list, stare intently at the screen.

Then she will close it again and clutch it tightly.

Rolands does call, but she is a distraction from Olivia's
indecision. Nevertheless, Olivia's attention is dragged back to
the case, as Rolands sees it.

"It would be good if you could do another press
conference," she says.

The media have not left speculation alone.

They report on unfounded sightings. They report on how

grief-stricken Olivia does or doesn't look. They speculate on her marriage, her mothering, and everything in between.

Talk-back radio shows take calls. It's always the women who are the vilest. Some part of Olivia floats above this, curious and speculating herself. *Is it that age-old, primitive response—if they other her enough, make her seem far removed from themselves, then they can't be tainted by whatever it is that Olivia is tainted with.* Photos of her where she is not a collapsed, sodden mess of tears are proof that she is not grieving like a "real" mother. A picture of Nick eating take-away alone instigates an entire thread of conjecture about her failings as a wife and wonder at whether these failings have pushed Nick into the arms of another woman.

It would be funny, if it were the subject matter for a thesis, or a comedy sketch, and not her life.

Occasionally, she scans these articles. They're always helpfully left in the center of her kitchen table, in newspapers that she and Nick never buy. The narrative is firmly pro-Nick and anti-Olivia.

"There's been some bad press," Rolands goes on, gently. "It's nothing personal. The media likes to have a good guy, and a bad one, that's all. Remember Lindy Chamberlain?"

Olivia understands; Rolands doesn't have to explain it to her. She's not weeping and begging in public spaces, feeding the public perception of how a mother should be. If people can blame her somehow, they think that they're protecting themselves. *That would never happen to MY child,* they think. *MY child is too loved/protected/cherished. MY child would not be neglected for long enough to be taken, plucked out of my garden. I am a better parent than THAT.*

At least at this point the story seems to be that she's too cold and focused on divorcing Nick to look after her child properly.

That's a narrative she can work with.

It's certainly better than the truth.

"When?" Olivia says now, in response to Rolands' comment. "Tomorrow morning?"

Olivia sighs her assent.

"We need to turn the narrative around. Make them see you as a person. Caring, distressed." Rolands is careful with her words, but the directive underneath is clear: don't be cold, don't be stoic. Be the terrified and grieving mother the public needs you to be.

Personally, Olivia thinks it's too late for that. Once the media has a story, it's hard to turn it on its head. People love a simple explanation: a good guy and a bad guy. Nick is too emotional and hapless to be the latter.

He's not effective enough to be viewed with suspicion.

"Does it matter?" she asks Rolands, wondering how public perception can possibly impact the police finding or not finding her child.

"Yes," Rolands replies, firmly. "It's a distraction. The media is focused on you. We want them working with us, helping us. Sending messages about what we want the public to be doing, what information might be useful, who might have some little tiny piece of the puzzle that might help us. At the moment, they're looking for pieces of the wrong puzzle."

Not really, Olivia thinks to herself. *Not as much as you think.*

But she jots down the details Rolands gives her, and agrees to brief Nick.

She can be the grieving mother the media needs.

She can be anything, now, she realizes with a start.

She's had enough practice.

23

———

THREE MONTHS Earlier

When Olivia thinks about the camping trip, she sometimes feels ashamed.

At other times, she feels the resolution of her convictions.

Today, the latter is at the fore.

It's no wonder things panned out the way they did, she thinks to herself, her hand on the kettle, waiting for it to boil.

It's the knowledge of Charlie's impending arrival: it has stirred up uncomfortable memories. To her credit, she doesn't blindly accept the explanations that paint her in the better light. Sometimes she examines the darker, murkier explanations. The ones where she has lost her mind a little bit.

Charlie has visited since that trip, of course. Patricia's time in London had stretched out and out, to Nick's rising frustration and Olivia's relief. It worked in her favor that Nick wasn't exactly a man of action, too: while he didn't like it, he also was never going to take any action to change it, and Olivia was grateful beyond measure.

Sometimes, in other contexts, she wished Nick was more

proficient at getting things done. But then she'd remember Charlie, and breathe deeply. And accept Nick as he was.

But now Charlie is on a plane. Patricia is dead, and it is a tragedy on more levels than Olivia could vocalize with anyone except Jodie. And while of course Nick was sad and worried about Charlie, and struggling to cope with all the practicalities, Charlie was nevertheless on a plane right now to come and live with them, and Nick was a little bit excited, too.

Olivia had agreed to trialling it—*what else could she do?*—but she knows that once Charlie has moved in, he will never move out. And something close to fear prickles at her. Fear that her equilibrium will be forever disrupted.

Fear that all the parenting disagreements she and Nick can barely resolve now will be exacerbated.

Fear that she will have to be extra careful, extra protective of Wolfie.

That she can't, in fact, be present with Wolfie and Charlie every minute of every day.

She needs to move on signing those documents, putting things in motion. But she feels panicked at the thought. She's not ready. She hasn't thought it through enough. She had thought perhaps it might not be necessary, that she could just forget the whole thing, but now Charlie's arrival is interfering with her plans.

And also, of course, she can't just forget it, and hope for the best. Things have been done, actions have been taken. They're not going to fix themselves. Doing nothing is not, actually, an option at all.

The kettle boils, and Olivia pours boiling water into her cup, forgetting to put a teabag in it. Later, she'll find the lukewarm water there and not remember pouring it. Her mind is at once empty and dazed, and racing blindly.

She has cleared out the spare room, made up the bed for Charlie.

She has placed clean towels, new soaps at the end of the bed.

She has asked Nick about Charlie's favorite meals and shopped diligently in order to prepare them—to help him to feel welcome and at home. She's even found the name of some grief counsellors, should he wish to talk to someone aside from them about his loss.

She goes through these motions, these tasks of welcome, of opening her home to her stepson, meticulously.

She thinks that if she makes the house just so, the bright new bedding and the cheerful plants that now decorate her spare room might conceal the less welcoming, dark recesses of her heart and of her thinking.

24

———

THREE MONTHS Earlier

Across town, Hannah stretches luxuriously in her expensive sheets.

Nick watches from the bathroom door, so she amps it up for his benefit: back arched, legs extending and writhing. Toes pointed.

Always toes pointed. Her mother taught her that. Though she meant it in a different, more demure context. A way to take a flattering photo, rather than a way to entice men into her bed.

The sheets are tousled between her legs, her shaggy red hair spread across the pillows.

She lets a low moan escape her lips.

Nick is beside her in an instant, the tie he was in the middle of tying ripped off and discarded on the floor.

"You drive me completely crazy," he mutters, reaching to pull the sheets away from her.

Her skin is creamy and soft, her breasts jutting upwards. He can't think clearly around her body.

Hannah, on the other hand, can always think clearly. On the topic of what she wants, at least.

And after much careful consideration, her thoughts have led her here: she wants Nick to leave his wife for her. She wants him to move in, ravish her, keep her happy.

She also wants to make Olivia a little bit unhappy.

Olivia is always so...superior. Always just a little bit too "holier than thou." Bringing Nick to his knees has the added benefit of bringing Olivia to her knees, too.

Hannah doesn't think too deeply about it; she wants, she chooses, she gets. If she thought a little harder, she might realize that her motivations are more about Olivia than they are about Nick.

But she doesn't think about any of this.

She moans again, and Nick's clothes are soon strewn across her bedroom floor for the second time that day.

"I want you to move in," she says. And when Nick stops his journey traversing down her body, abruptly, shocked, she pushes him gently back into motion.

Getting men moving in the direction she requires is her specialty.

AFTER NICK HAS GONE, Hannah surveys her handiwork smugly.

Her bedroom is a mess. Sheets and clothes are strewn everywhere. Her favorite bra is—bizarrely—hanging from the corner of the shower door.

And soon, Nick will be living here with her, able to fulfil her desires on a daily basis.

Olivia might not be talking to her—again—but she has ways and means of getting her attention.

Stealing her husband, for a start.

Honestly, it was easier than she could have imagined. Nick was putty in her hands.

To be fair, though, Olivia hadn't really helped herself. She'd pressed Hannah to have Nick over to draw up some plans for a full reno on her apartment: luxury kitchen, luxury everything. Hannah couldn't really afford it, to be honest, but Olivia had been so encouraging, she'd thought, "What can it hurt?" A free consult with a talented architect...who happened to be extremely pleasant to look at, to boot.

That was after the falling out, the years of not talking. Hannah had put it down to guilt—Olivia trying to make it up to her, by offering up her husband. *In more ways than she'd bargained for*, Hannah had thought and smirked to herself.

Oh, she shouldn't have done it, sure. She didn't really know why she did. *Habit?* In all honesty, she'd missed Olivia. She was grateful to have her back. But it seemed almost like this plot line was written in the stars—she was powerless to fight it. It was like a play unfolding on the stage before her eyes. Nick coming over in the evenings after work. Loosening his tie, accepting a glass of wine. Even before he started drawing up plans, he'd be wandering around the house with Hannah, measuring things, asking about her dreams, her desires. And somehow one day those desires had spilled out from describing sumptuous bathtubs a woman could luxuriate in, with floor-to-ceiling tiles in tasteful hues, to describing him pressing her against a wall, one thigh between hers, his lips on her neck. His breath hot in her ear.

It *could* have been scripted, it was so inevitable and perfect and steamy and divine.

So, now she has Olivia *and* Nick.

Well. She thinks she does. Olivia hasn't been replying to her messages, again. But she hasn't made any of her grand statements about needing space, or Hannah being a bad person, or whatever, either. Not like that last time. So Hannah thinks it is probably okay.

She knows it can only be "okay" for as long as Olivia is oblivious, however.

Oblivious Olivia.

Something about the impending fallout feels a little bit exciting to Hannah. Nick had been evasive about how and when, but it doesn't occur to Hannah that she would ask Nick to move in, and he wouldn't comply. And while she pretends to wrestle with how difficult it's going to be when Olivia finds out where Nick is going, she nevertheless is humming with low-grade anticipation.

She guesses this will get Olivia talking to her, again.

Honestly, she can't keep up with Olivia's moods and proclivities. She isn't even that interested in finding out why this time. The last time was utterly ridiculous. Olivia had declared that she, Hannah, was an emotionally violent person and she chose not to have her in her life anymore. And she'd cut off all contact without so much as a backward glance.

Perhaps that was why Hannah had strayed into Nick's underpants. *She wasn't a bad person.* Perhaps she was just hurting about that injury all those years ago. Over nothing. Nothing! They'd had a little tiff, was all. They'd all said hurtful things. *That happens, in families.*

As Hannah mulls over this, justifying her betrayal in a few surprising heartbeats, she hears her phone beep, and leaves the subject with a sense of finality. She is untroubled by the need to think about things too deeply, or to consider her contribution to the situation. She is quite impressively comfortable with blaming Olivia, and taking no responsibility herself.

"Bing." The message reads.

Speak of the devil.

A month after Hannah had texted her, though.

Olivia and her bloody moods.

Who takes a month to reply to a text message?

Still: Hannah is eager to see what she has to say. She opens her messages, and laughs a little at what she reads:

"Step-parenting is harder than you think."

25

Sunday

The afternoon stretches into evening, and Olivia hasn't gotten out of bed for the entire day.

At one point, Nick quietly takes her in some tinned soup. He knows she won't eat it; she's gone limp with distress. He knows that food will only make her feel nauseous. But he wants her to feel cared about anyway. To know that he is thinking about her. That he wants to nourish her, in some small way. Because he can't do it in the one way that matters. He can't bring Wolfie back.

He wishes she would eat. She's becoming smaller and smaller in front of his eyes. He'd slipped an arm around her in bed the night before, and been shocked at her protruding hips. Her belly was hollowed out, concave. He thought that if he held her too tightly, she might break in half.

She'd acknowledged the soup, then rolled back the other way, staring at the wall.

She's been sleeping so badly. Her thoughts are like an old-fashioned newsreel, flitting from one picture to another, with white static and clumsy editing. Now, the camping trip is playing in front of her eyes. But she's not quite sure what is reality and what are just her worst fears.

Did this happen? Did that?

Vaguely, she remembers that after the camping trip, things changed.

It wasn't that Nick loved Olivia less, really. Not in the long term. He could separate out the events of that week and put them in an "other" box—anomalies that didn't fit into his regular life, his marriage. He viewed them as a glitch, an error.

Olivia's error.

But he didn't see them as anything bigger. He didn't see them as the things that sowed the seeds of everything that came after. Everything that led them to…now.

Olivia could almost read his mind, as he settled back in to their ordinary lives.

Olivia made a mistake.

She was stressed, and she shouldn't have been drinking.

It was a one-off.

He didn't need to do anything more about it; the matter was closed.

It was, in fact, Olivia whose thinking did a U-turn that week. While Nick would maintain that she was in the wrong, that she lost her way momentarily, she herself saw things that she couldn't un-see.

The way that Nick failed to see nuance in a situation, for example.

The way that he was blinded by love.

Not just love for Charlie. Love for her, too.

And mainly, the terrifying way that things might look for her child if she was ever out of the picture.

Olivia's eyes are closed, but she can see it like it was yesterday.

Wolfie was playing on the floor with his favorite truck. He was murmuring to himself, zooming the truck hither and thither, smiling, engrossed.

And Charlie, as he had been doing all week, seemed to need to insert himself into the picture. He couldn't seem to exist without someone paying him attention—usually Wolfie. Olivia was frustrated: she wanted Wolfie to play independently. She actively encouraged it. It was a relief when he became so absorbed in his own games that half an hour would pass in blessed silence. No demands, no questions.

No bodily contact.

It wasn't that Olivia didn't love Wolfie touching her. His little body was so perfect. His skin was so smooth and soft, his affection so exuberant; having him in her arms was the closest thing she experienced to bliss. But at the same time, the physical demands of parenting surprised her. Without enough time experiencing her own personal space, uninterrupted, something inside her got chipped away at. Never with Wolfie. But with Nick, standing behind her and wrapping his arms around her waist; or even colleagues at work, leaning close to look at her monitor, talk about her project. All of it made her stiffen slightly, as though she could push them out of her personal space through the sheer force of her body language alone.

She soaked up Wolfie being occupied with something else, her physical being slowly relaxing. It was *regulating,* even. She needed it, like she needed air.

And Charlie. Charlie needed something else from her child. At its most basic level, she would have said he got a little self-esteem boost from Wolfie's attention, from his laughter. *And what was so bad about that? He was seeing his little half-*

brother, who he was lucky to see once a year. Who wouldn't want to spend as much time as possible, soaking up his adoration?

But something about it made Olivia uncomfortable. It was hard to put her finger on; even harder to try to express to Nick.

There was something in the way that Charlie watched Wolfie. It was a shrewd expression, glancing from Wolfie's face, to the toy he was playing with. He looked older than thirteen. It wasn't the simple joy of a thirteen-year-old boy, wanting to join in some game that was bringing someone else happiness. It wasn't jealousy: wanting some of the joy being experienced by another. It wasn't even wanting to take the joy solely for himself.

If Olivia had to stake her life on her interpretation, she would say that *Charlie wanted to take Wolfie's happiness away.*

He'd insert himself, too close to Wolfie, and start talking about or doing something else to take his attention away from the item that was bringing him such pleasure. Usually, his interruptions were strange plays toward making Wolfie whinge or nag. Reminding him of something he wanted but didn't have.

And then when Wolfie was irritable and demanding, he'd slip back away, suggest he and Nick go for a walk or hit the cricket ball around, leaving Olivia with a cantankerous toddler.

The first few times, Olivia tried to be generous.

He doesn't know how to play with a toddler.

He's just trying to get his attention and be involved.

He just wants to feel part of things.

But by the end of the week, Olivia had had enough.

She'd tried to raise it with Nick, in a hushed voice in bed once she was sure the kids were both asleep. But he'd been dismissive, saying to her the exact same things she'd been saying to herself all week. When she'd pushed it, saying, "I'm actually quite worried about it. It doesn't fit with how other thirteen-year-olds behave. It's making me quite stressed," Nick had become irritated. "Stop making problems where there aren't any," he'd snapped. "He's a great kid, trying to entertain a toddler and help us out. Why can't you just be generous for a change?"

Olivia had instinctively curled inward, away from Nick in the dark, her stomach tensing almost to the point of cramping. She was grateful the pitch black afforded by their campsite: even with the stars, she could not make out Nick's silhouette, and so knew he could not make out hers, either. She opened her mouth, struggling to control her tears in the dark, desperate, for some reason, that Nick should not know how deeply he had wounded her. He didn't seem to care about her distress in relation to the kids; it felt too vulnerable to have him know how deeply his words cut her more generally.

Was she not generous?

Olivia tried to find a place for this assessment in her own perceptions about herself. On the surface, she felt she could list a whole host of actions she had taken in relation to Charlie that seemed to her to be above and beyond "generous." She had devoted hours to the practical tasks of co-parenting when she and Nick had shared care of Charlie. She had thought about parenting; she had read books. She'd reached out to other parents to ask how to best instigate a bedtime routine when there was none, and how to cope with the fallout. She suffered cups of tea with Patricia, who was smug and superior and, Olivia suspected, deeply insecure: one of those people who have to list their achievements to you at your first meeting, without you asking anything even vaguely related to that topic.

Charlie had taken up swathes of her time, her money, and her emotional energy.

And yet...

She knew that deep inside, she *was* less generous. She had wished Charlie would just vanish, on many occasions. One day, when he was seven, she was lying in bed with Nick, a rare morning that Charlie hadn't woken them before six. Waking up naturally, stretching and snuggling, a thought had crossed her mind so dark and so terrible she'd sat up in alarm.

Maybe he died.

Nick had startled, propping himself up on one elbow, rubbing his eyes. "What is it?" he'd asked, and Olivia had struggled to mask the confusion and shock she had felt at her own thinking. "It's 7.30," she'd replied. "Charlie isn't up. I just had a moment of worry that something was wrong. He never sleeps this late."

She'd lain back down slowly, staring at the ceiling, that unbidden thought staying with her all day.

Somewhere, in her subconscious, a thought occurred, for the first but not the last time: *was she a monster?*

Later, another question gets added to it.

Was she a monster?

Or was he?

26

___

OLIVIA AND BING *huddle behind their closed door.*

They share a room, still.

Olivia is eight, and she doesn't mind at all. Bing is ten, and she wants her own room.

From behind the closed door, they can hear things breaking.

They are not afraid. In fact, it is usually one or the other of them who can reach Abby, through the noise and confusion. Olivia, in particular, is finely attuned to him. She can see when he is starting to not cope. She can even predict it, if anyone cared to listen to her.

But her parents are overwhelmed and they are not listening.

Today, they had been watching the television—a rare treat in daylight hours. Olivia could feel Abby shifting restlessly beside her. She knows if they turn the volume down and all sit quietly, he will be fine. But her father is grumbling in the background—he prefers children outdoors, not underfoot, on a Saturday afternoon. Her mother is washing dishes, banging pots and pans. Cutlery scrapes and clanks in the bottom of the sink.

The neighbor's dog is barking incessantly.

Olivia starts to shift in her seat, too.

Then her father is upon them—he has just seen the state of their rooms. Olivia feels guilty, because it is really her and Bing's room that is the problem. Abby's room is always neater.

Her father yells at them to turn the television off until their rooms are clean. Her mother pops her head around the corner, soap suds dripping from her hands.

"Leave them alone, Daniel. They're just having a rest." She glares at her husband: she, too, has at least some sense of when Abby will be pushed out of silence and into something different.

But Daniel is a father of the times—he has spoken, so action must follow. The nuances of his son's ability to cope with particular situations are lost on him. Olivia tries, tentatively, to redirect him: "Please, Daddy. Abby needs some quiet."

Abby is starting to rock ever so slightly backward and forward on his chair. Olivia feels desperate. It is so subtle, but it is almost too late.

"Please," she whispers again, hoping her tone and volume will be contagious, that her father will catch on. "Abby's room is tidy. Leave him, and Bing and I will go do ours."

But Daniel sees an opportunity different to the one that Olivia sees: "Fine. He can do the mowing. He's been shirking helping out for years and he's certainly big enough and old enough to do some more chores."

Daniel isn't a bad father. He loves his children in the way fathers in the eighties loved their children—in small doses, with restrained affection, and little involvement in their day-to-day lives.

His son, however, perplexes him. Abby is effeminate, at odds with his oversize frame. He's more childlike than expected, playing happily with Olivia and her dolls quietly for hours. He is physically awkward, his large limbs getting in each other's way. He still can't catch a ball, if he was even inclined to try.

And then—inexplicably, when Daniel tries to tie all these things together and form a coherent picture of who his son is—there are the rages.

Today, Daniel is in a bad mood. He wants to watch the cricket, and resents Amelia's decision to let the kids watch television. He wants them to go play outside, and leave him in peace. And like many others before and after him, when he doesn't understand something, he simply rejects it.

Abby starts to shake his head: no, no, no, no, no.

"Excuse me?" Daniel says, his eyebrows shooting up in disbelief at this outright defiance. His irritation grows. "I've shown you how to do it a hundred times. I'll start it for you. Come on!"

Olivia starts to panic. How does her father not see what is going to happen? It is as obvious to her as the sun rising in the morning.

"It's too loud for him, Daddy!" she squeaks, pulling at his sleeve, desperate to have him look at her, sure she can convey to him the severity of the situation with her eyes alone. She can't believe this is happening.

Again.

"Rubbish!" Daniel says crossly, pulling his arm out of Olivia's meagre grip. "He needs to toughen up, that's all." Here, he reaches over to grab Abby's arm. Abby has started to softly tap his forehead with the palm of his hand. The sound is rhythmical.

Tap, tap, tap.

Daniel grabs the tapping arm, and pulls Abby to his feet.

"Mum!" Olivia yells, wincing at her contribution to the noise and the confusion, but needing someone to stop her father. And then Amelia is there, yelling too, and Abby frees himself from Daniel's grip and crouches down next to the table, his hands over his ears, rocking more wildly. His head starts banging into the leg of the table.

Crack. Crack. Crack.

The thumps hurt Olivia, too.

Then there is shouting, grabbing, pushing, pulling.

And Olivia knows what is coming, and she grabs Bing's hand, and they run to their room.

27

____

SUNDAY

Olivia startles. Was she dreaming?

She's lying in bed, clutching her phone.

Memories swirl and float around her, just out of reach.

Bing.

They had been a team once, Olivia thinks. But it's hard to remember. Flashes of her childhood come to her at random moments, leaving her breathless, her heart pounding. Something bad lurks there, but it takes her a while to remember what it is.

Now, Olivia thinks about her relationship with Bing. When they stopped talking completely, Wolfie was about to turn one, and Olivia was happy.

Sometimes, when she's half awake, the familiar dark feeling she associates with being a child pushes down on her relentlessly. *Something bad was here.* She can never quite place her finger on what it is. She thinks she remembers—*she and Bing are estranged. Of course it feels bad.* But there's always an unsettling feeling underneath. Of that not being quite it, either.

Now, it's dark. Olivia is aware that she hasn't gotten out of bed all day. She needs to talk to Nick about the press conference. She needs to eat something, but the thought turns her stomach.

She thinks she'll just lie in bed for a little bit longer.

Her thoughts turn back to Bing. Those bad feelings. She presses around in them, trying to find the bruise, to explain the darkness that flutters just outside her reach.

She'd been avoiding Bing all year. But she'd made an exception for Wolfie's birthday.

To an outsider, it was nothing: the merest of misunderstanding, so innocuous as to render the outcome staggering. It was nothing compared to some of the earlier grievances.

Like the time that Olivia had shyly confessed to Bing about Dale, the boy she had a crush on at school. Only fifteen, it was her first real experience of infatuation. Dale was tall and sporty and popular and there was no possibility that he would notice Olivia, let alone date her. So when she heard through the grapevine that he'd been making out with Bing at his older brother's birthday party, she justified the betrayal away: *it was not as though she had any chance with Dale. It was not as though Bing was taking something that was hers.*

She never mentioned it to Bing; but she never told her who she had a crush on again, either.

And then there was the time when she had had a fight with her boyfriend, Ash—long gone and happily forgotten. He'd been controlling and jealous and he drank too much, and one night in the rage only experienced by the powerless, Olivia had thrown all his expensive wineglasses against the wall.

It was not a moment she was proud of—the thought still makes her cringe, at who she'd let herself become with him. But she understood it. The cycle of drinking, and jealousy, and control. The feeling of being utterly, utterly powerless to change anything or break out of the cycle. And even as she did it, she knew it wouldn't help anything: it was a child-like solution to a very adult problem. *If I break your glasses, you can't drink and you can't get crazy and controlling and we just won't get into this cycle again, will we? And then we can live happily ever after, can't we? CAN'T WE?*

But knowing it wouldn't help didn't stop it feeling really good. One tiny little sliver of power in a world where she had none.

She and Ash broke up not long after that. She'd shared the story with Bing in tears: her shame, her helplessness. The realization that she couldn't change Ash; she could only leave.

Months later, at a family lunch, Bing had thrown it up as a casual anecdote about Olivia's temper, laughing about "that time you broke all the wineglasses" in front of their family and friends. Olivia had just started dating Nick—it was his first introduction to her whole family. The occasion was stressful enough, without Bing belittling her in front of everyone.

It wasn't so much that that information was now public knowledge: Olivia had worked through that experience in such a way that made sense to her. She would never be proud of it, but she could explain it in a way that allowed her to forgive herself. What hurt was Bing's motivations. *Had she wanted to make Olivia look bad in front of her new boyfriend? In front of their parents?*

And of course Olivia felt foolish: she trusted Bing again and again, and Bing constantly let her down. She felt gutted and lonely.

But she always forgave her. She always let her back in.

Always gave her room to wield her knives and slice Olivia.

Because it might not be good for her, and it might always hurt her, but she remembers a different Bing. She had nearly ten whole years of a kind sister, a loving sister, a sister who looked out for her.

Even thirty years of a different Bing later, it was hard to cut off the part of her that loved her sister. It was hard not to keep hoping for something better.

Even when she thinks about the fight.

She had been up late, getting things ready for Wolfie's party. It was just a small event: her parents, Bing, Jodie and Maggie, and one other mother and child Olivia had met at Story Time at the library.

In her usual manner, Bing had expansively declared that she would make the cake. Olivia was cautiously grateful: Bing would make a great cake. But she also might just as easily get caught up in something else and forget about it. Olivia had learnt from experience that Bing was very busy, and very important—although for the life of her, Olivia could not keep up with what her job was from one year to the next. Making commitments and sticking to them was not Bing's greatest strength. On top of that, she'd been keeping her distance from Bing all year; the offer seemed incongruous with the reality of their relationship. While she hadn't stated to Bing anything directly, her lack of availability and interest in connecting must have been obvious.

Mustn't it?

It was curious to consider that for all Olivia's inner turmoil about cutting off contact with Bing, that Bing might, in fact, have not even noticed the difference.

So she'd texted her two days before the party, reminding her that Wolfie was obsessed with trains and trucks, and asking if that train from the Women's Weekly cake book would be too much work, as she herself would be happy to make it if Bing didn't have time.

Bing had never replied.

So at 11 p.m. the night before, she'd sent—admittedly, a slightly snappy—message saying that as she hadn't heard back from her, and the party was at 11 a.m. the next day, she would pick something up from the cake shop.

She was disappointed for Wolfie—he would have loved that damn train—but mostly disappointed in herself. She should know better than to rely on Bing. *How many times had she been let down? And how many times did she go back for more?*

She was especially annoyed with herself because it impacted Wolfie. She knew it wasn't a big deal: Wolfie would love any cake. But she didn't want him to be affected by her failure to learn that she could not rely on her sister. Not for the little things, and certainly not for anything bigger.

Still—her text message certainly hadn't been awful. Occasionally, even now, she scrolls back to it, to check. To reassure herself. *I'm not insane. It didn't say what Bing thought it said.*

Sometimes she shows it to someone else, just to check, too, because she knows that everyone gets things wrong. Everyone perceives things differently. *Is it possible to believe this was a violent attack?* she will ask them. Jodie, for a start. Her mother. Her therapist, who she saw for a year afterwards, trying to untangle her thoughts and feelings about her sister.

I'm upset that you haven't got back to me to let me know, the text reads. *Wolfie's first cake is important to me. I'm going to go to the cake shop in the morning to pick something up.*

She'd gone to bed without giving it another thought. Secretly, to be honest, she was hoping she'd wake to an apologetic text: *So sorry! I thought I'd replied! Cake is all done and good to go! See you at 11!*

Instead, she woke to something else.

Now, Olivia closes her eyes. Her head hurts. Her heart hurts.

Her mind wanders.

Olivia is seven, and her big brother is playing peek-a-boo with her.

She's too old for peek-a-boo, but never too old for attention from

Abby. He's like dessert, the chocolate frog in the jelly, the special treat you only get every now and then so you savor it.

Every. Last. Piece.

He's large for his age, and awkward. His face is big and round, like a friendly sun. When Olivia draws pictures on the kitchen table, her suns, in fact, always look a little bit like Abby.

When Olivia thinks about him now, however, she can't quite remember what is fact and what is fiction.

She can't check with her parents—even after all these years, she knows better than to ask them any questions.

But she remembers feeling loved, and she chooses to hold on to that.

28

———

MONDAY

Hannah feels sorry for Olivia.

This is unexpected: she would have expected to feel a little gleeful when things don't turn out quite so perfectly for her perfect little sister.

But the media have it all wrong. Nick isn't with her because Olivia is a dud: that narrative doesn't sit well with Hannah at all. There's no competition if there's no competition. She wants to have won this particular race because she is the better lover, not because Olivia couldn't even get out the gates.

The news coverage, in fact, is pissing Hannah off. She will be remembered not as the seductive, glorious victor, but as the girl mopping up someone else's slops. This whole new storyline makes Nick considerably less attractive to her—no longer a prized possession to be fought over and conquered... but her little sister's discarded husband, perhaps not even valued by Olivia at all.

Was Olivia seeking a divorce?

Hannah does not even really care about the truth. She cares about the perception that will taint her relationship with Nick.

Until Wolfie disappeared, they were working toward Nick leaving Olivia and moving in with her. And now that end goal seems decidedly less shiny.

And here she is now—God, she's everywhere: Hannah sees Olivia's pale, striking face on her muted television. She has a moment of indignation and thinks to turn it off, but she's too curious. She turns up the volume.

Olivia looks uncomfortable behind the podium. She's surprised they have her standing; she looks awkward and ill at ease. She looks, in fact, kind of sickly. Nick is beside her, trying too hard to look warm and loving. One arm is stiffly around Olivia's waist. The presenter is asking them about their marriage: "So there's no rift, no talk with lawyers about divorce?"

"No," Olivia says, but she's so faint she's barely audible. She clears her throat. "No," she says, more firmly. "Nick is a wonderful father and husband. He's been such a rock through this time. He's kept us positive—" Here Olivia chokes up a little, clutching for Nick's hand. She allows herself to look down, be overcome by her emotions, and Hannah guesses—correctly— that she's been told to show her feelings more. "I'm drowning in my fears and he is keeping us all afloat," she gasps, starting to sob.

Nick looks down at his wife. Even with stubble and dark circles under his eyes, he's a strikingly attractive man. Now, his eyes are soft and loving, genuinely. He looks touched by Olivia's words, and Hannah throws her keys at the television, cursing.

God, he's an idiot, she thinks. *Is he really falling for that?*

She hasn't noticed, and would stridently deny all the tricks and ruses she's used to manipulate and captivate him, like asking him to move in with her while he's distracted by her writhing hips, so she sighs in frustration, snatching her keys back up from the floor. She briefly searches the screen for damage, and turns it off, just as she sees Olivia collapse into Nick's arms, and him wave further questions away, leading his wife tenderly from the podium.

AFTER THE PRESS CONFERENCE, Nick and Olivia lie together on the couch. It feels to Nick like the most genuine intimacy they've shared in months. Olivia is lying along the length of him, resting lightly against his body, her head on his shoulder. They're quiet. They don't have a lot of words to say.

"That went well," Rolands had said, nodding encouragingly, after Nick helped Olivia from the stage. Olivia was quiet then, too—she had seemed exhausted beyond any capacity to converse further. She had let Nick speak for her, and take her home.

Journalists had followed them. They lurked around their driveway, where they'd been ever since the story on Olivia visiting Paul's offices, trying to get quotes or snap pictures, getting in the way. Olivia pretended she didn't see them: gave them no air time at all. Nick smiled apologetically, tried to be friendly, tried not to get anyone offside.

They had both warned Charlie, categorically, not to speak to any of them.

Now, he comes in the door, whistling. He startles when he sees them both, lying quietly, two pairs of eyes falling on him, a silent heaviness permeating the room.

Even Nick, it seems, has run out of words to say.

"Hi," says Charlie, awkward. He tries to tuck a newspaper inconspicuously further under his arm.

"Why are you buying that rubbish?"

Nick's voice seems far, far away to Olivia. But she's glad someone is asking Charlie that question.

"I'm just trying to keep up to date," he falters. "About Wolfie. I miss him, too, you know."

Nick shifts next to Olivia, sits up, puts his head in his hands. He rubs at his temples. "Of course, kiddo. I know it's a really hard time to be here. You've been so helpful. It's just...the articles are upsetting. And that's not a reputable news source. So do you mind keeping them out of the house, please?"

Charlie's face is expressionless, but he nods, and tosses the paper in the bin on his way out of the room.

Olivia watches his retreating back. She tries to remember the camping trip, again. Her mind is playing tricks on her: she can't quite remember what is fact and what is fiction. She's too hungry to think clearly, but the thought of food makes her stomach turn.

She remembers watching Charlie more closely on that last night.

Damper. They were eating damper. It was a tradition that Nick relished, but the dough always tasted too heavy, too cloying for Olivia. The thought now makes saliva rush to her mouth, as though she might be sick.

They were sitting around the campfire, the sun setting past the trees.

In the distance, she could hear birds warbling, the creek running lightly over rocks.

Or was it rain on the canopy roof she was hearing?

She can see them around the campfire; but she can also see them huddled under the shade sail, hiding from the rain.

Olivia shakes her head, trying to clear it. *Sunset and campfire, not rain.* She's almost sure of it.

Nick was explaining something about fishing to his son. Olivia wasn't listening to the details; she's not interested in fishing. She was interested in Charlie's expressions of emotion. Or lack thereof.

Charlie was watching Nick, with that blank expression Olivia saw so often, nodding and making noises of assent. Olivia got the sense that he was humoring Nick—that Charlie was not very interested in fishing either.

It's nice that he's trying to be involved in Nick's interests, Olivia had thought to herself, in direct opposition with the more vocal, less charitable thoughts that were pressing in. But when Nick paused and glanced up at Charlie's face, Olivia watched Charlie fumble for the right line. "It's really special getting this time with you and the family," Charlie said. "I've really missed you while I've been away."

Nick had glowed, and patted Charlie's knee. He made some touched response that Olivia tuned out. She was watching Charlie carefully.

She remembers his blank face, the light from the flames dancing on it eerily. She had searched his face for the emotion beneath this statement, but it looked rote, rehearsed, a learnt response that was not coming from anywhere inside Charlie. At Nick's response, he looked satisfied, like he just received a good grade, or at least a pass, rather than that he just shared a moment of intimacy or connection with his father.

Olivia watched and doubted herself.

Why was she obsessing over the emotional world of a thirteen-year-old? Weren't they all stumbling their way through, learning to regulate and understand their emotions?

What is wrong with her?

Her thoughts reflect the firelight: flickering, transient. Burning a little bit. She remembers a very strong desire to pack Wolfie up and take him away from this child.

He's a child, she caught herself, though. *Isn't it up to me to teach him, to guide him, if I see things that Nick doesn't see?*

But even without having the words to articulate it, she knew that if Nick saw it differently, her ability to influence the situation was limited. He'd made it very clear that it was "his child; his decisions." On some level, Olivia even knew that Nick probably equated this with love: he loved Charlie more, so he would make the best decisions for him.

Olivia saw *that* differently: that that in itself influenced her capacity to love her stepson. That night, by the campfire, it seemed like an intricate and delicate web that even with all the thought and attention she paid to it, Olivia herself couldn't figure out. Some days, step-parenting felt so impossible that it broke her mind: all she was left with was jagged, empty space. She couldn't compute that anyone had done it successfully. It seemed as incredible as space travel, as living on Mars.

Her desire to flee was primal: she sensed danger for her child, and then shame at her own response to her stepchild. Nevertheless, she just wanted to snatch Wolfie up and take him far, far away. Forever.

At the same time, she couldn't find any words to express what was troubling her. Once, she tried to talk to Jodie about it, and stumbled over her words, her worries sounding lame and trite.

I don't think he feels anything.

He says what he thinks he's supposed to say, not anything authentic.

There's something...cold about him.

Jodie had tried to understand, to explore further, but Olivia had had nothing further to add. She could see the confusion in Jodie's face, her desire to support and understand her friend, but also her failure to understand. To see the problem that Olivia saw.

She hadn't tried to explain it further. She knew it sounded ridiculous. A child who hides his emotions is hardly the most unusual thing in the world.

A thirteen-year-old not playing well with a toddler sounded perfectly reasonable when she said it out loud. *How much experience do teens have to practice such a thing? Why on earth did she expect it to be better?*

Still, a whole week in each other's space like that. From nothing, to everything, in a one-room tent.

What did Nick really expect to happen?

29

Monday, Week Two

Charlie sits in his room, surveying his handiwork.

The articles are cut out neatly and are arranged in chronological order on the pinboard that he asked Nick to buy for him.

They're all from the trashy papers that his father has asked him not to bring into the house, but Charlie reasons they are out of sight—they can't upset Olivia in his bedroom.

A couple of photos are circled in pink highlighter: these are the photos that he has supplied. He knows he's not supposed to talk to the journalists, but he likes being involved. He likes feeling he is contributing something.

Also, the reporter had been so interested, so grateful. He'd also slipped Charlie a couple of hundred-dollar notes, which was thrilling somehow.

Now, though, there is a soft rap on the door, and Charlie has not considered this possibility—that Nick or Olivia might come into his room to speak to him.

He stands up hastily, and goes to the door, opening it just

enough to converse with his father, who looks grey, and smaller than Charlie remembers.

He himself has grown a lot, but Nick has shrunk somewhat too. Not in reality, but in his stance, the defeated air around him. The jovial, chatty man Charlie arrived to just three short months ago has vanished.

"Just checking in," Nick says now. His eyes rest on Charlie. He's trying to be a good dad, trying to remember all the things he has to do, but there's a blankness behind his eyes Charlie has never seen before.

Charlie puts a hand awkwardly on Nick's shoulder. "How are you, Dad?" he asks.

"Things are pretty hard, huh?" he goes on, when Nick doesn't answer.

Nick, for his part, feels a pang of regret, or shame, even. Charlie has lost his mother—his whole life in London. He's living in a new place, with no friends, no supports. Except Nick, who is barely holding things together. And Olivia, who does her best, but well. *She's not really been a great stepmother, has she?* She certainly wasn't upset when Charlie moved to London, and didn't really keep in touch with him at all.

And then there was all that rage that came out on the camping trip.

Something whirs away in the back of Nick's mind.

All those years that Olivia and Hannah weren't talking. He hadn't really paid that much attention. Hannah hadn't seemed like his type of person, then. She was loud. Brash, even. They'd never spent that much time together, even before Olivia had told him she wanted to limit how much time they spent with Hannah. But now he remembers something about Hannah criticizing Olivia's step-parenting. How gutted Olivia had been.

The memory unsettles him. Somehow, it makes his infidelity worse. That he's cheating on Olivia with someone who had hurt her so badly; and also that his thinking just aligned with Hannah's, like it was two against one. Until that moment, Nick would have resolutely maintained that he was on Olivia's team.

Feeling suddenly sick, Nick sees for the first time how delusional this is.

Hannah and Olivia were reconciled by the time he slept with Hannah; it was Olivia, in fact, who'd pushed him into helping her. Now, that memory nags at him uncomfortably too. His irritation with Olivia. She and Bing had only just started talking again. Olivia had been evasive about the details. Hannah was out of their lives, for years. Then suddenly she was back in them, and she was everywhere, and Nick was supposed to give up his evenings to help her?

He'd resented the renovation project. He thought Hannah was just as demanding and entitled as ever.

He honestly couldn't say that he'd seen anything in Hannah that would make Olivia trust her again. Nick knows that her trust is hard won.

Why had Olivia decided to let Hannah back in to their lives?

But then there'd been the long evenings, chatting renovation plans over cold wine. Hannah had been so much more interested in his ideas than Olivia had been, when he'd tried to share them. Hannah had been more interested in everything that came out of his mouth, to be honest. Olivia had been cold, and distant, even though Nick was doing *her* a favor.

The differences between the two sisters had been so stark: Olivia, cold and harsh and dismissive and uninterested. Hannah, so warm and teasing and interested and...available.

There was that word, again.

Nick would hate to think that he could be led astray by someone merely being warm and available. When he thought about it, back then, at the start, he added other layers: how attentive Hannah was; how she remembered things that were important to him, that Olivia forgot. How curious she was about how Charlie was doing; how Nick felt about his absence. He had contorted some common niceties into something more, so he could tell himself how he clicked with Hannah, how connected they were. And he glossed over the fact that he would never have looked twice at her had she not whispered something erotic in his ear one night, and turned him on.

Now, though, he sees that for what it is: entitled, self-serving.

If he loves Olivia so much, why would he do that to her? To them?

And as this internal cacophony crashes into his consciousness, all the things that he's refused to think about since Wolfie's birth are suddenly, starkly, apparent.

Olivia's obsession with parenting.

How, once Wolfie was born, Nick wasn't her number one anymore.

How that tapped into what Patricia had done, making him doubt his value, his worthiness.

And how instead of trying to work it out, talk about it, deal with it, he'd shoved it deep, deep down and let it control his choices, his motivation, such that Hannah stroking his ego a little bit had seemed like the answer, instead of the worst thing he could possibly do to feel better.

30

———

RAY LEARNS *how to survive in dark places.*

Sleep. Wake. Beg. Forage.

Hide.

Johnny keeps pretty quiet on the whole, but gives him tips on where to sleep and how to survive in the new world in which he finds himself. He learns which cafes are lucrative when begging for food scraps, and which bins local grocery stores dump waste in at the end of each day.

He learns tricks for keeping warm, and what to say to police officers who come through to move them on from time to time.

He doesn't think to tell the police what he'd seen his father do to his mother, or that his father had grabbed him afterwards, dragging him, screaming and crying, taking him who knows where, to do who knows what. He doesn't think to ask what has happened to his father. He has vague memories of his mother calling the police, once? Twice? And them not helping her. Not helping her at all.

It does not occur to him for even one moment that the police could help him.

The only person who has ever helped him through this mess is Johnny.

Life falls into a comforting pattern. Sleep. Wake. Beg. Forage. Occasionally older boys and men try to make trouble, but Ray has become proficient in finding places to hide.

He sticks close to Johnny. The older man doesn't seem to mind. He's not inclined to make small talk, but he'll talk about the things that matter. He'll look out for him, and share food when Ray has failed to find any. Once, he asked Ray—gently, carefully—where his family was, and images rushed into his mind: screaming, shoving. His mother's eyes the last time that she looked at him. He was just a boy, but he could see that her terror was only partly for herself—the rest of it was for him, her boy, about to be alone on the balcony with that man.

That man.

He had crumpled then, the tears hot and violent, bursting out of him for the first time since that day. Being dragged downstairs, thrown in the car, everything getting darker and smaller and more painful by the minute. And after that, blackness. Till Johnny.

Warm hands reach for him in the gloom. It's the only time Johnny has touched him, and being held makes everything worse, not better, because he remembers everything that he once had, and now has lost.

31

TUESDAY, *Week Two*

The police want to talk to Olivia again, and she is nervous.

How can a child disappear without a trace? the media ponder, forgetting history; forgetting how often this has actually happened.

In the space between a good story and reality, Nick and Olivia exist, suspended.

Olivia is gaunt, hounded. She has given up all pretence of coping, and stays in bed. She doesn't even cry anymore. She just seems to be sinking. Nick imagines he might go in there one day and she will have vanished into the bedsprings completely. But he's not managing much better. Charlie speaks to him, and he does not even hear: his eyes are vacant, his shoulders slumped in palpable, painful defeat.

Neither expected this ordeal to last for a week. Both have completely exhausted any means they have to cope. They move through the house like spirits, the presence of the other a gentle puff of air, gently dislodging one another, so weightless they have become.

Theories abound: pedophile rings; maternal filicide. An

elaborate kidnapping plot to frame Nick and punish him for misdeeds the public do not believe he could possibly have committed.

But Olivia was there.

Olivia, they think, *knows exactly what went on.*

Olivia is too pretty and too silent to be innocent.

"WE SPOKE TO PAUL O'BRIEN," Rolands says, watching Olivia carefully.

Nick is with her, one hand on hers, but the gesture is no longer protective. He does not emanate warmth and strength. *He seems*, Rolands thinks to herself, *even less present than Olivia.*

"Oh, yes," Olivia says. She tries to sound curious, but her attempt falls flat. Her mind is elsewhere. Even the flash of nerves has passed. She no longer cares what Rolands thinks or doesn't think.

"Patricia left Wolfie two hundred thousand dollars," she goes on, her eyes still fixed on Olivia, who doesn't respond at all.

Nick, however, stiffens beside her.

"What?" he says.

Rolands shifts her gaze to him. He looks like he is trying to drag himself out of somewhere heavy and hazy, struggling to make sense of Rolands' words.

"Did you know about this?" she asks him, but turns her gaze back to Olivia. Her eyes flick to Nick sporadically.

Nick glances at Olivia. "You said a few thousand," he says. There's no malice, or even any curiosity in his words; he has registered the peculiarity of this information, but confusion is his main response.

His son is still missing. His fears are crushing his chest. His culpability in choosing what was easy over what was right is suddenly, starkly clear to him, and memories of Patricia, so well-buried until now, are flashing before his eyes, blindsiding him with the pain and the force of them.

He can barely breathe, let alone compute complex information or ascertain anyone's motives in this instance.

Nevertheless, something nags at the back of his mind. Something not quite right, an elusive memory just out of his reach. Something about money and his wife. He tries to chase the thought, pin it down, but it skips out of his reach, and his attention is drawn back to the present.

"What happens now?" Olivia asks. She's staring blankly off to the side, disinterested. Whatever plans were attached to this inheritance previously, she is unmoved by them now. They don't, in fact, even seem to exist in the same reality that she currently inhabits.

Rolands drones on about trust accounts and signatories. These things take time. There's administration. A whole lot of administration. Olivia and Nick need to sign things, set up accounts, talk to the executor. Most of this information drifts over Olivia's head. For all her earlier planning, she can't remember anything of the sort—*did Paul explain to her all these steps and complications?*

It's all moot now, anyway.

The money was to provide for Wolfie.

And Wolfie is gone.

32

___

THE FINAL DAY of their camping trip, Olivia had screamed at Charlie.

It wasn't a rebuke; it wasn't losing her temper a little, like she sometimes did with Wolfie.

It was screaming, and hatred, and rage.

She had risen early. She loved watching the sunlight dance on the leaves of the gum trees. With everyone else asleep, she could lie back in her camping chair with her eyes half closed and listen to the birds and the sounds of the bush.

She'd already been down to the river to get some creek water to boil for their morning tea. Wolfie was curled up in bed with Nick—he'd crawled into Olivia's side of the bed at some point in the night, his warm little body curling into her. He smelt like a baby still, all warm skin and baby shampoo and something earthy and wholesome. Olivia didn't want to encourage sleeping in her bed, but she secretly loved it and found it hard to direct him back to his own. Even on the small mattress she was sharing with Nick camping, she loved his delightful little body next to hers. The expansiveness of him: the way he flung his arms about in his sleep as though to take in the whole world. On a physical level, it did not make for the greatest night's sleep—but on an emotional level, something about that carefree ownership of her, and her bed, and the world, melted her heart.

When Nick and Charlie finally stirred, Olivia felt refreshed. An hour of solitude did that for her: reset her worries, her agitation, the splintery feeling she got when too many things were coming at her at once. Sixty whole minutes of the birds and the sunlight and the stillness had soothed parts of her that she didn't know were agitated.

It was a new day. Charlie would be going back to London in just a few more days—Olivia wanted to try harder. Her worries and her negativity felt burdensome. She thought that she could actually feel the changes in the lines around her mouth, getting more and more set into a stern, stiff, unbecoming frown. Nick had caught her expression in a photo, and she had recoiled slightly. *When did she become so negative, so...old?* She didn't even recognize herself.

A good night's sleep—even with a toddler in her bed—and some natural beauty and solitude filled her with vigor. She would be a better stepmother. She would understand and guide and if there were corrections to be made, she would make them with love and gentleness.

She would unset her mouth from that rigid, hard line.

She handed Nick and Charlie a cup of tea each, smiling benevolently. She felt so full of love and lightness. Nick had smiled at her appreciatively, leaning in for a kiss, as though he could see the change in her already.

Life looked so full of promise.

Later, she would tell Jodie that it felt a little like losing her mind.

To anyone watching, it would have *looked* like losing her mind. All the dark thoughts that she had harbored, and tended, and fretted over all week were not banished by a morning of solitude, as she had imagined: they were churning inside her head, dampened down but not eliminated. Trapped in a tent with no privacy and no one to unpack them with, they were in fact festering and growing and wrapping around everything. And for all her goodwill and calm that morning, it was now late afternoon. Olivia had been sipping chardonnay and nibbling biscuits for an hour, or was it two? Never a big drinker, the tight coil of angry, suspicious, resentful thoughts loosened, along with her tongue.

Charlie did what he'd been doing all week: he inserted himself into Wolfie's solo game, upset him, and removed himself. And Olivia was certain she saw the hint of a smile as he turned away.

Wolfie was sobbing on the floor, the truck he had been tending to so lovingly discarded. Somehow, Charlie had taken away its shine. More than that: he'd rendered it worse than joyless, an object of pitiable worthlessness.

Perhaps it reminded Olivia of Bing: a lifetime of someone taking the sunshine out of everything. Someone claiming to love you, while secretly, furtively always trying to make it rain over your head. Maybe that was the trigger, the thing that she couldn't bear.

The thing that made her snap.

Olivia had been preparing them a snack; she hadn't heard the exchange that preceded his change in mood. She had turned toward them at the first wail, and had seen Wolfie throw the truck aside, the despair on his little face palpable.

Something about the discarded truck caught in her throat.

How did a thirteen-year-old manage to take the joy out of an object, adored a minute earlier, so completely that she could see its lack of value in the angle of Wolfie's face, turned now away from it, like he couldn't even bear to look at it?

It wasn't just that though: Wolfie's crumpled little face said so much more to her. He had no words for it, but he could grasp the murkiness of Charlie's intentions. She saw the injury right there in his face: the confusion as to why his beloved big brother would make him feel bad.

She didn't even need to ascertain the details.

Charlie had upset Wolfie. On purpose. For his own pleasure.

"Get back here!" she had screamed at Charlie's retreating back, and he'd turned back to her, shocked. "Why do you keep doing that?" she'd continued, shouting, letting all the hatred and fury she'd spent all week—years, really—concealing, spill across her features with unrealized relief. Her animosity was cartoonish, monstrous, a shifting, brown, gruesome shape she could almost see as she shouted and spat.

She felt like a blocked hose, the blockage finally dislodged, her wrath writhing and bucking and spraying indiscriminately, everywhere. And she had no control over it whatsoever.

What's wrong with you?

Why do you like to make my child unhappy?

It's evil, you're evil, get away from him! Go back to London, I don't want you here! I don't ever want you near my child again!

Nick had come running, glaring at her, leading Charlie away, his turn to be furious now, their angry exchange in front of both children ricocheting around the trees, and Olivia had felt drunk, and devastated, and so, so alone.

"You're imagining it," Nick had hissed, turning his back on her. Comforting Charlie.

They'd eaten dinner in silence, then Nick had packed up the tent, banging and hurling and muttering to himself, driving them all home a day early, fury emanating off him in the harsh, hard way he moved, in the glances thrown at her as he did so.

"Don't you ever speak to my son like that again," he'd said, clearly and purposefully, right in front of Charlie, as they pulled into their drive.

That night, he had slept on the couch.

But after that night—miraculously, unbelievably—things went back to normal.

It was hard to fathom. Olivia kept waiting for the fallout, some consequences, her life to fall apart. And it...didn't.

Nick carried on the way he'd always done. He was busy at work, and loving at home. He was tired, but rushed straight in the door to bathe Wolfie and read him bedtime stories, delighting in fatherhood in a way that was somehow intensified after camping. After the first night, he was back in their bed without so much as a telling look or a frosty, turned back.

He didn't go so far as to suggest that he'd work part-time to share in the day-to-day parenting, but he was fully present and engaged when he was home. And he did more than a lot of other fathers, Olivia reasoned to herself.

He didn't seem, in fact, to have been affected by the camping trip at all. He started talking about another baby, his eyes glowing. Olivia was confused. Had he not seen the gaping rift between their ideas of good parenting? Between their ideas of what was appropriate behavior and what was not?

For the second time in her life, she was ashamed of her conduct. She turned it and twisted it this way and that, trying to make sense of it—and she could, to some degree.

She was alone with her worries and fears.

Nick dismissed them, dismissed her.

He assumed his interpretation of everything was correct; it didn't even occur to him to consider that she was right, and he was wrong. It didn't even warrant a conversation.

Camping was a pressure-cooker of heightened emotions.

She was drunk.

She should not have been drunk with the children.

But she also knew that something had shifted between her and Charlie, and her and Nick, that could not be shifted back.

Nick was oblivious. Or was he? Sometimes, she had the disconcerting idea that Nick had decided he would love her, and so everything he saw was through that lens: committed to her, believing in her. This was so set in stone that he didn't need to—and therefore didn't—examine it or think about it or reassess it. He loved her, and he would readjust everything to accommodate that.

Even when the evidence of her deserving such faith was under question.

The thought unsettles Olivia. It makes their relationship feel fixed, rigid—like Nick might not be engaging with reality, but some airbrushed, shiny version of her that isn't real. She can't quite put her finger on it. It's comforting to be accepted for who you are, sure, but this seemed to go one step further. *Is he afraid that she won't love him if he isn't one hundred percent supportive, one hundred percent of the time?*

It wasn't always like this. Like so many things, she thinks things changed when Wolfie was born. *Was it laziness? Was he just too tired to engage with complexity anymore?*

Did he just not care? Was this superficial version of themselves as a couple good enough for him?

She had tried to talk to him about it, but he was always resolutely positive: he was happy, they were happy, life was good.

Olivia thought it was disconnected with reality somehow.

But besides that, life *was* good.

Patricia had extended her contract by a year in London, again. Nick was devastated, and Olivia was overjoyed. She focused her energy on Wolfie, and work, and without the pressing issue of Charlie between them, she could even relax into loving Nick more freely too.

He wasn't quite what she had imagined in those early days. Later, she had learnt that there is research about this: that when you meet someone, you're basically high. Your brain releases a chemical cocktail that in effect means you're making decisions about a potential life partner while tripping off your head. And she does think she saw Nick through I-want-to-settle-down-and-have-kids-one-day glasses: he was so committed to Charlie. He got down on the floor and played with him for hours, like no man Olivia had ever seen. He loved him stupendously. He answered his questions thoughtfully.

He was nothing, nothing like her own father.

She was hopelessly smitten.

And her, well. They'd lie on the couch on the nights they didn't have Charlie, talking through each other's designs and projects, talking about what they wanted in their futures. In their families.

Now, Olivia is acutely conscious of all the things they didn't talk about. Who would work? Who would look after children? What did they each think about discipline and additional support and healthy eating and screen time? The big picture—well their dreams and desires converged and soared, a kaleidoscope of beauty and wonder and possibilities without limit.

It was the day-to-day stuff they never bothered to talk about.

The little, inconsequential things that did, indeed, have consequences.

33

———

Olivia cries when Abby leaves.

Her mother has told her, over and over again, that he is going to a special school where he will be able to learn all the important things that she is learning at school: things that he can't learn currently, at her school, because he disrupts the class and the teachers can't teach.

At night, eavesdropping, stealthy, Olivia hears other phrases —"difficult behavior," "violent outbursts," "unmanageable."

Olivia is torn.

She has seen Abby at school. Her bumbling, good-natured big brother turns into someone else. He lurks and crouches. So kind and smiley at home, with her, at school he is angry and mean. He trips the other boys over. He once slammed Michael's head into a wall.

But Olivia sees why, too: the way the other children taunt him. The way he is excluded. His odd way of moving, his hulking size; the way he doesn't meet anyone's eyes. The way he tries to share the chocolate cake in his lunch box—his hopeful, misplaced, heartbreaking attempts to make friends.

At recess and lunchtime, Olivia rushes to find her brother. She will take him to a far corner of the playground and sit with him, play *finger figures, hum softly. Often, they don't even talk. She feels responsible for him. She just wants him to have a sliver of kindness and quiet in his days.*

Sometimes she cannot find him, and on those days, she listens furtively to the whispered conversations between her parents: what the school said. What had happened.

Her little heart rails at the unfairness of it—but it turns toward hopefulness, too.

Might Abby make some friends in this new, special school?

Might he be happier there?

Bing is nowhere to be seen in the playground. If any adults were watching, they might notice how hard Olivia works to save her brother: from loneliness, from bullying, from hurting. Even at eight, Olivia understands that Abby is different to the other kids. Mostly, she wants to protect him from their jibes and cruelty.

They might also notice how hard Bing works to pretend it is not happening—to shut it out. How she sets up her entire days so she doesn't have to see it.

But no one is paying much attention.

Occasionally, Olivia wishes Abby would just be normal so she could go and play skipping or tag with her friends, shrieking and running around madly and being eight. So even though she feels, deeply, that sending him away somewhere else will not fix things, and not help things, she's a little bit relieved, too.

A little bit unburdened.

So she holds on to her hope that everything will get better, even while knowing, instinctively, that they will actually get worse.

34

Two Months Earlier

Have you told Olivia yet?

Hannah hits send on the text message without thinking. She's finding it hard to wait.

She wonders what things will look like with Olivia once Nick is living with her. What the fallout will look like. She thinks back to the last fallout. She was only trying to help her little sister, for God's sake. Just like she always did. And Olivia—pre-emptively—had attacked her for being slack.

It escapes Hannah's notice that she had in fact forgotten to make the cake for Wolfie's birthday. So if she ever thought self-critically about it, she would see things differently than the narrative she holds on to tightly, with such conviction. *We all said hurtful things,* she told herself at the time. Sure, she'd texted, *Don't try to blame me cause you failed to organize your kid a cake.* She might have even said something mean about Charlie, about how Olivia had never made him a cake. But Olivia had called her a "bad sister," a "shit person," "despicable." Though once, when she had scrolled back through the messages to show Nick how crazy his wife was, how vicious and violent, she couldn't find the ones that said those things. All she saw were flashes of her own words, with enough ugly words, enough animosity, enough flashes of twenty-year-old grievances that were irrelevant to the discussion—all of them on her side of the conversation—to not want Nick to see them, and to not want to ever have to see them again herself. So she abruptly told him there was no point holding on to bad energy, and deleted the whole conversation—years and years of text messages to her sister.

"I want to remember the good parts of my sister," she'd told Nick as she did so, breezily, like she was the better person, and they'd both let it go without a challenge, without another word about it. When Hannah mentions the estrangement to any friends, she tells the same story—how vicious, how violent Olivia's messages were. How she'd had to delete them so as not to have to accidentally see them ever again.

"They were unspeakable," she'd said, solemnly, and after a few recitations of this, even she believes it as the truth.

So she was self-righteous and gratified when Olivia reached out to her. It was the way it should be: Olivia caused the problem. She should grovel a little to fix it.

They hadn't spoken for two-and-a-half years. Wolfie was now three-and-a-half, and Bing had no idea who he was or even what he looked like.

***

BING WILL REWRITE THIS HISTORY, too, however: a couple of short years later, she will recount to their mother that *she was the bigger person—she reached out to Olivia to make amends*. She will even add in little details, mindboggling, random, and untrue: that she left a homemade fruit cake on Olivia's doorstep. That she received no response, so she followed it up with an email, saying she missed Olivia; asking for a cup of tea.

It's not a malicious lie: Bing truly believes that this is what happened. When their mother raises this with Olivia in good faith—*It was nice of Bing to make a fruit cake for you, as an olive branch, wasn't it?*—Olivia is stunned into silence.

Intuitively, she understands that it is not propaganda, but a reflection of the way that Bing exists in the world. She remembers once, when Abby had been gone for months, clutching his favorite teddy bear and crying—and Hannah had tried to soothe her, saying, "He's happy at the new school, Liv. He told me about his new friends, all the things he's learning. It's better that he's there. He's going to do better." And Olivia had stared at her sister, stared and stared, scrolling through her memories of every last weekend with Abby, wondering where such a sentence could possibly have fitted. All she had seen was sadness, hopelessness, defeat.

Was Hannah trying to make me feel better, or herself? Olivia had wondered. She didn't think that Hannah could possibly be so blind to reality that she believed such a thing. And it wouldn't be the last time she'd see her sister will a new reality into existence by the sheer force of her need for it to be so.

After the fruit cake comment, Olivia had thought about how it was possible to exist in the world with so much certainty. Most people doubt themselves at least a little bit. At least on occasion. And even if you don't doubt yourself, Olivia mused after that conversation with her mother, most people have good friends who can pull them up when they go too far. Give them a reality check. She doesn't always like it, but Jodie will raise an eyebrow, tilt her head to the side. If necessary, she'll tell Olivia she's out of line.

"Er, I think you're wrong about that," she'd said, that time that Olivia suggested Wolfie's anxiety—new, confusing—was related to the rift with Bing. Olivia saw it, instantly, of course. She was getting herself so worked up about things, about the cause, about what had happened. She was looking for someone to blame. Her thinking was spiralling madly. But as soon as Jodie said it, Olivia could see the insanity of the idea. She had breathed deeply, looked at Jodie sheepishly. "Oh, yeah," she'd said, and they'd both laughed. Or, "Really, dude?" when Olivia pitched her theory about Nick's tendency to ignore Wolfie while he was reading the paper. She had genuinely thought for a few minutes there that he was punishing Wolfie, trying to make Wolfie learn, through his rigid silence, to leave him alone.

Some people think good friends see the world the way you do, so they agree with you and cheer you on, and to some extent Olivia thinks this is true. But *really* good friends know your insanities even better than you do yourself.

Did Hannah not have any close friends who she could be honest with? Who could help her be honest with herself?

Really good friends will tell you when you're straying too far off the path.

Really good friends will stop you, before you do something crazy.

Or they would, if you happened to share your crazy plans.

Olivia startles. She'd always been able to be honest with Jodie.

But she hadn't been honest recently, had she?

Perhaps that was where Olivia went wrong. She knew she was straying a little too far from reasonable.

She knew someone would stop her.

So she kept her agenda completely to herself.

35

Two Months Earlier

Charlie moves around the house methodically.

Wolfie trots after him. "What are you doing, Cho-cho?" he asks.

"Just seeing what the house is like," Charlie replies.

Olivia drifts behind them. She feels like a crazy person: she can't sit with a cup of tea, she can't watch something on the television, she is stuck in this cycle of supervising her child, seeing nothing to worry about, berating herself, then seeing something that she worries about very much indeed.

She had expected more tears, more grief from Charlie—and then when she reflects on this, she wonders why. His strange emotional world is one of the things that she has always noticed about Charlie.

On her better days—her hopeful, caring, proactive days—she wonders if he is on the spectrum. She suggested to Nick an assessment, and he waved her concerns away. He did not see anything unusual about Charlie. Olivia felt dismissed and began to doubt herself.

Was she imagining it?

On the days where she can't shake her fears, her worries, other diagnoses float to the forefront of her mind.

Sociopath.

Psycho.

Today, Wolfie seems calm. It's his first week with no childcare, his first week home with Olivia, and she resents sharing him with Charlie. She resents having to parent two kids, instead of one.

She resents having to be diligent. To not be able to tune out, now and then.

She can't talk to Nick about this. She is afraid he will dismiss her, again, and she will feel less and less like they are on the same team.

But Charlie starts school tomorrow. The weight that drapes across her, rough and bleak and suffocating, is close to lifting. At least most days, it will be just Wolfie and her.

She's jealous of how Wolfie has taken to Charlie. He adores his big brother. He looks at him much like Olivia remembers looking at Bing: as though he is the sun. As though his warmth and light are the whole world.

She fears for Wolfie, loving someone like that. Siblings might look like warmth, but you shouldn't trust them just because they're related to you by blood.

There are many things about Charlie that remind Olivia of Bing.

Charlie treats him like a toy—he'll use him for his own amusement when it suits him, then discard him, walking away from him without a word, without an explanation, and shut his bedroom door in Wolfie's face. And Wolfie will come to Olivia, distraught, longing for more of Charlie, and it eats away at her, enraging her.

Charlie does nothing to deserve Wolfie's love.

He is not kind or thoughtful or gentle. He will recruit Wolfie for his own agenda, then leave him hanging. And Olivia hates that Wolfie loves Charlie. But love him he does—so she wants Charlie to be careful with Wolfie's precious little heart.

Today, she is conscious of hovering. *Does Charlie notice?* she wonders. *Does he understand why? Or is he oblivious?*

Charlie instructs Wolfie to get him some string and paper: he's going to make the boy a toy.

Wolfie is delighted, running in little circles, making the strange little clucking noise he makes when he is happy.

Olivia is torn between joy that Wolfie is happy—it happens so rarely these days—and trepidation. Because she knows Charlie will lose interest, and disappoint Wolfie. And Wolfie will not be able to understand what follows.

Now, Charlie sits on the floor. Wolfie is asking him, over and over, what he is making.

"You'll just have to wait and see," says Charlie, making his eyes big and wild, egging Wolfie's excitement on. "But it's going to be very special! And very BIG!" Here he holds his hands wide, showing the grandeur of his project, the size of Wolfie's expected joy.

Wolfie plops down beside him, clapping his hands together gleefully.

"What color? What color?" he asks, his eyes fixed on Charlie, his little face rapturous.

Charlie could cut out a circle, and Wolfie would be overjoyed.

Olivia observes all this, her heart unable to settle. Part of her is sour, resentful (*she* could not cut out a circle and it be received with joy. Wolfie expects more of *her*). But part of her longs for Wolfie's love and attention to be reciprocated genuinely; for him to bask in the love of his big brother, and be content.

She swings wildly between these two states, overlaid with apprehension—she has seen this play out enough times to know that Wolfie's satisfaction will be thwarted. Charlie likes arresting his attention—feeling the full strength of Wolfie's adoration and attentiveness. He loses interest in the follow through. The payoff for him is at the start: knowing Wolfie is hanging on his every word.

Now Charlie is cutting a large circle out of purple cardboard. He has a pile of other colors beside him, and he continues building up the anticipation.

"It will be beautiful! And fierce! And *special*," Charlie tells Wolfie, as he cuts and threads.

A green triangle.

An orange claw.

"You can take it to the park. You can *play* with it!"

Wolfie claps and gurgles, his words jumbled in nonsense sounds in his excitement.

"You can even scare your mother with it," Charlie whispers, conspiratorial.

He glances at Olivia here, and winks, and her heart lurches.

Is she meant to join in the game, pretend to be frightened by the end product?

But she and Charlie both know there will be no end product.

Or does he not know? Olivia wonders, again. *Does he genuinely lose interest, and not realize he has repeated this pattern ad nauseam since he arrived?*

Wolfie is on his feet again, jumping up and down, giddy with longing to see what Charlie will build.

Then Charlie sighs heavily, puts the scissors and the cardboard down.

"I'll finish it later," he says, not even glancing at Wolfie. And he stands up and goes to sit on the couch. He reaches for the remote, starts flicking idly through channels. Wolfie is devastated, trotting after him, pawing at his legs.

"Cho-cho? Cho-cho?" he is saying, his voice full of longing. "When? When?"

Charlie doesn't even answer. He starts watching some news. He has tuned Wolfie out completely. It is as though Wolfie does not even exist.

Olivia catches Wolfie's hand.

"I'll finish it!" she exclaims, expressing excitement she does not feel; trying her hardest to not allow Wolfie to feel this abject disappointment, again. To distract him, bring him back to joy.

It's not that he is missing out on the toy that Charlie was building, she thinks to herself.

She's trying to shore him up against the knowledge that Charlie does not really care for him. That Wolfie's needs are irrelevant, inconsequential: somehow, Charlie's need to feel important has been met, and Wolfie's distress does not move him. Does not touch him at all.

Wolfie follows Olivia back to the cardboard, but his disposition is confused and pained.

She can't protect him from what he perceives. Even in his little, four-year-old mind, he knows that the completion of the toy will not fix things: he knows his big brother has discarded him, and his little heart hurts.

"No TV in the daytime," she says to Charlie sharply, without looking at him, and he looks at her—bemused—and shrugs. Then lopes off to his room.

36

———

Tuesday, *Week Two*

Olivia still sometimes reads Bing's messages from that morning, years ago.

It's like a scab that she can't stop worrying: she knows it is unhelpful, and painful, and she does it anyway.

Sometimes she tells herself it's a reminder—a reminder of all the reasons she can't trust Bing. All the reasons cutting her out of Olivia's life was the right decision.

It's also a justification. Though Olivia doesn't think about it that way.

She had just been expressing disappointment—and, okay, anger—about a goddamn cake. It wasn't meant to be an assessment of Bing's entire person.

Is a bubble bursting about someone always so...slow? Olivia wonders. It felt like an exhalation, rather than a pop. She'd already cut Bing out of her emotional world, for the most part. She'd thought she'd put Bing somewhere that she couldn't hurt her anymore. But Bing's claws were apparently hulk-like—big and strong and razor-sharp, they could reach anywhere. In her mind's eye, she sees Bing like the lion in *The Clan of the Cave*

Bear: determined, stretching, straining to meet their mark. To sink into flesh.

To draw blood.

To eat her alive, maybe.

Except that lion gives up, goes on to other things.

In the aftermath, Olivia had tried to understand. She'd posited theories to Nick, stretched her brain as thin and wiry as was possible for her, contorting to find her way into the places that Bing's mind obviously occupied. But in the end, she could make no sense of it.

Just because your life is shit, you want to make me feel bad too?

I told you you'd be bad at mothering. You can't even organize your kid a fucking cake.

I feel sorry for Wolfie having you as a mum.

Did you even ever make Charlie a cake? Don't pretend you care about children.

On and on they went, all day. By the end of the day, Olivia had equated the sound of her text messages to violence and pain. She had to block Bing, and change the text tone. Even then, it took her a full week to stop the flash of panic every time she heard her phone ping.

Now, though, nothing feels the way it was supposed to feel.

She was supposed to have solved this problem: killed two birds with one stone, as they say.

It had taken planning and undeserved kindness and problem-solving and months.

It had taken *pretending*.

It had gone against everything she knew to be true: that Bing was bad for her, and would savage her again, one day.

That Bing was not to be trusted.

Mostly that Bing would be so self-righteous and smug about a reconciliation, when she deserved to be so much less.

But Olivia had the bigger picture to think about. She had comforted herself with the notion that though Bing would feel like she won, it would in fact be Olivia who won in the end. And at the time, she seemed to get from point A to point B to point C effortlessly, and her plan had seemed perfectly reasonable. Now, though, her heart lurches at the thought.

Was it parenting that did this to her?

Was she this crazy before she had a child?

She tries to remember life before Wolfie. Before the little gaps between her ideas about parenting and Nick's ideas became chasms, impossible to traverse safely. She wonders if Nick—dependable, optimistic Nick—had even noticed any changes in her. She had always kept somewhat to herself—but at some point, this had distorted into *secretiveness*.

Now, she's trying to claw her way back from the precipice. She feels like a foreign creature, a black, enormous spider, all scrabbling legs and beady eyes.

She had wanted Bing to take her husband off her hands.

She had wanted that edge in the issue of custody.

She had mused one day how easy it would be to propel Bing and Nick into each other's arms—how predictable they were. How easily manipulated. And once the thought occurred to her, it seemed so small, so easy to orchestrate. She had been so *curious*.

Could she really pull it off?

She had wanted to take Wolfie far, far away from both Charlie *and* Nick.

She had wanted a perfect little life for her and Wolfie, and she had completely lost her mind.

37

———

Tuesday, *Week Two*

The familiar *beep, beep, beep* of ABC news rouses Ray from his memories, and he listens nervously for news of Wolfie Hitchens, the missing little Melbourne boy. It's been the lead story all week.

He's only an hour away from home, after eight long days on the road. His heart is in his mouth as the news is covered. Only a minute or so of air time is given to Wolfie.

Still missing.

No leads.

The presenter urges anyone with information to call Crime Stoppers, and Ray wonders if he could call them. But what would he say?

That he knows where lost little boys end up?

Thinking about it makes Ray's chest tight. He tries to think about something else.

Getting home. He's been teaching his partner to drive. There has been much resistance, but Ray has insisted: *"Just say something happens to me? Just say there's an emergency?"*

Ray actually worries that it's too late. Can you teach a forty-four-year-old to drive a car? The lessons are painfully slow. But Ray is a good teacher. He's patient, and knows how to speak calmly, softly. He's already taught his partner enough of the basics of reading and writing to do some simple things. Even when he's panicking slightly himself, he can keep his voice low, soothing.

He tries to think about what to focus on for their next lesson. But his mind keeps drifting back to the police, to the Hitchens boy.

Little boys, without their mothers. Alone in a world full of dark places and dark hearts.

Ray is having trouble breathing. His vision starts to blur slightly. He's on a tight schedule, he mustn't stop, but he has to stop, the truck brakes screeching and groaning as he swerves into a parking bay, too fast. Gravels sprays out from his wheels, and he gasps for breath, the blackness engulfing him, obliterating the vision of little boys with golden curls into nothing but darkness, unreachable and out of sight.

38

———————

"BUT WHY DOES *he have to* stay *there?" Olivia whines.*

Amelia is peeling carrots and potatoes. The house is eerily quiet. It's Abby's first week at his new school—he leaves on Monday mornings and comes back on Saturday mornings. The concept is terrifying to Olivia.

Isn't he lonely?

Who will read him stories at bedtime?

Who will help him if he's hurt?

"It's just how the school works," Amelia says, not looking at her daughter. Olivia is voicing all the fears that she is trying to push away. "They say it will help him to settle in, get used to the new routine."

"He'll be back before you know it," she adds.

Olivia is perched on a stool behind the breakfast bar. She sits quietly, the pain in her chest growing and growing since Abby was taken.

Taken.

He'd been screaming and crying. There'd been grabbing and holding.

Forcing.

As Olivia watched, stricken, all her hopes for Abby about the new school seeped quietly away.

It's Tuesday night, and the whole family is quiet.

At dinner, Olivia glances over and over at where Abby would usually sit.

There's an aching hole in her heart, but her family sees it differently.

Daniel almost seeps into his chair with relief: dinner is a peaceful affair. There is no fighting, no angry outbursts, no refusal to eat, no melodramatic dry retching and gagging. No punishments.

No exhaustion.

Bing is in her element: in this new empty space, she regales her parents with tales of her day. The niggling discomfort she feels about her brother's absence is shoved deep down, and covered over with layers and layers of shinier things.

Even Amelia seems to move about through one long, deep sigh of relief. Dinner is made, served, eaten, and cleaned up.

Everyone gets ready quietly for bed.

It's their brave new world, and she clings on to what the adults tell her: that it is better, and right, and will all be okay.

On Sunday afternoons, *Olivia glues herself to her brother's side, and tries to shore him up with enough family love to last him the whole week he'll be away.*

After the first weekend, she doesn't comment on the bruises she sees on his arms and back. One on his temple, even.

That first weekend, though, she'd shrieked. Abby had startled wildly, arcing away from her, his toothbrush sailing through the air. Olivia had caught herself, shushed herself. She asked Abby about the bruises, but he seemed more distant than usual. He gently pushed her out of the bathroom, and got dressed in there, alone.

She had marched into her parents' bedroom, alerting them

forcefully of this new and terrible information: "Someone is hurting him! He's got bruises everywhere! The school must be horrible. You've got to get him back." Bolstered by her childlike belief in right and wrong, she had assumed her parents would fix everything, and nothing more needed to be said. So when they bundled Abby back into the car to return there on Monday morning—there was less screaming this time—her little eight-year-old heart was wild with indignation and disbelief. She had stomped her feet and refused to get in the car when she realized Abby was not, in fact, coming back to school with her, but would be dropped back at his new school after she and Bing were dropped off at theirs.

Amelia looked uncomfortable. Olivia even wondered if her mother was going to cry. But if she was so upset about it, why was she taking him back?

Her father was terse, though. He seemed craggy to Olivia, his face grey and worn. Olivia couldn't remember the last time that he'd played with her.

Bing crawled into the back seat beside Abby with a book and an air of disinterest. If she worried about their brother, Olivia didn't see it. And as she stomped and wailed, her father grabbed her by the shoulder and shoved her roughly into the car. Olivia was so startled that she stopped wailing mid-cry. Despite all the fighting, the breakages, the throwing and screaming, Olivia was not afraid of her father. He'd smacked her on the bottom on the odd occasion, but only when she'd done something very naughty, and she had almost expected it.

This was different: she felt the unfairness of it in her bones.

She was just trying to look out for her brother.

Which no one else seemed to be doing.

Why did that her make her father angry with her?

Later, on the road, she started to weep quietly to herself: no longer a protest about Abby's fate, but a silent recalibration of what and who her family was; and what was to become of them.

39

———

One Month Earlier

"And you filed a report, how many years ago?"

"Thirty-one." Amelia Shorten pauses for a long time. Then: "And thirty. And twenty-nine. And twenty-eight. And—" Daniel shushes his wife gently. Amelia is trembling. It's always this way when they come to the station. He knows that she looks fearful, but really she is shaking with rage. Partly she is enraged that no one has been held accountable. No one has ever shouldered any of the blame.

Partly she is shaking with rage at herself.

Now, she stares down at her hands, resting lightly on the plastic countertop next to the screen that separates her from the police officer tapping away at her computer on the other side.

The station had been surprisingly busy. She sat with Daniel stiffly in the waiting area, worrying at her fingers.

They waited for half an hour in real time; but in reality they have been waiting for thirty-one years. Every year, on this date, they come back. Or they did. They've missed a few years. It's only fanned the flames of Amelia's rage.

So many people to not forgive, and not forget.

Most especially herself.

The police officer taps away at her computer, taking details, searching for things.

"I'll look into it," is all she says. "Someone will call you," as she gestures for them to leave the room.

Amelia and Daniel return home, the silence deafening. Between them, behind them, are thirty years full of children and holidays and career successes and their modest Sydney residence, close enough to the beach to retire in.

There is also thirty years of missing Abby.

They don't talk about it. They don't even cry about it. But every year, on the same date, they get dressed, and get ready, and drive to their local police station without having to say a single word.

40

———

TUESDAY, *Week Two*

Detective Rolands leans back in her chair and closes her eyes.

It's supposed to be her day off, but she can't shake the case from her mind.

How does a four-year-old vanish without a trace? No one heard anything, no one saw anything, no one has any idea where he might be. And despite a flood of calls to Crime Stoppers, nothing of any substance whatsoever has been reported by the community.

Rolands ponders Olivia.

There's something that she's holding back, Rolands knows, but she can't put her finger on what it is. There's some guilt in there, for a start. *But that's normal.* Wolfie was in her care. Any mother would feel guilty. It doesn't take that much time to lose a child, really. If you turned your back in a shopping center for thirty seconds, you could lose them. Maybe for five minutes, if there were no sinister characters about. Maybe for longer, if there were.

Whatever the circumstances, you'd still feel guilty.

So Rolands doesn't want to make too much of the flashes of guilt she sees on Olivia's face every now and then.

She's interested in the money. Nick and Olivia seem comfortable, but not wealthy. So she doubts that Olivia truly forgot about two hundred thousand dollars. *And what of the inheritance itself? What a strange occurrence*, she muses. With a very basic investigation, it seemed that Patricia was very wealthy. Her parents had a huge import/export business that Patricia had sold when they both passed on. And even though Nick and Patricia's split appeared quite amicable on the surface, it was still more than unusual for money to be left to his child with another woman. Rolands has never heard of anything like it. *Were the two things connected, somehow?*

But there was no ransom. And the money itself was still tied up in administration. It's not like it was sitting in a bank account somewhere, ready to be pulled out at a moment's notice.

And what about Charlie?

He would come into a great deal of wealth on his twenty-first birthday. But that seemed to have no bearing on the case whatsoever—it was far too far away to be useful. Olivia had worried about how he would be with Wolfie, there was some fears there, some mistrust, but Charlie was at school when Wolfie went missing, the school have confirmed he attended all his classes that day. Anyway, a teenager being a murderer or complicit somehow...well, it seemed a bit far-fetched. *What could possibly motivate him?* And he hadn't been in Australia long enough to have made plans, found an accomplice, really, had he?

Her thoughts run on. *When did Wolfie's anxiety start? Had something happened with Charlie? Before he moved here, at a previous visit? Sexual abuse, for example, could result in serious mental health complications for a child. Maybe Charlie didn't take Wolfie, but maybe he wasn't completely innocent, either.*

A knock on her door interrupts her train of thought.

"Cuppa?" Macy holds out a steaming mug toward her, and Rolands smiles at her wife.

"Thank you," she says, reaching for it, reaching for Macy's other hand, too, and giving it a squeeze. Macy is used to their free time being compromised by her job. Today, they had intended to go for lunch at a new winery that had opened down on the Peninsula, but Rolands is preoccupied.

Macy understands. A missing child is a sensitive area. So they don't need to speak about it. Macy cancels their reservation. She books again in a few weeks' time. She hopes and hopes that Wolfie will be found safely and returned to his parents by then. She is extra thoughtful, extra kind to her wife.

Rolands continues to think. She makes the odd phone call. There's the whiff of a marriage on the rocks, but no one is talking much about that. Maybe the flashes of guilt she sees in Olivia are not about losing her child, but to do with her marriage. She'd considered that Olivia had hidden Wolfie and was going to make off with the money, but it wasn't enough money to start a new life. She'd get more from selling her half of the family home she shared with Nick. And besides, where would she have hidden him? *And what sort of mother would traumatize their child by hiding them away from everyone they know and love for*—she glances down at her desk calendar —*nine days?*

No, that wasn't worth following. There was *something* about this family, though. A troubled child. A difficult blended family circumstance. Some dissatisfaction in the marriage. A weird inheritance.

Rolands exhales slowly.

Then she reaches for the phone.

41

———

TUESDAY, *Week Two*

Olivia huddles into Nick on the couch.

Unspoken, it is where they head now. Minutes tick by, hours.

Olivia curses herself.

When the chips are down, it is Nick who she wants to be with. She is surprised to find that here, the length of his body against hers, is the only place that she finds some comfort.

The outside world presses in on her, but on the couch, nestled into Nick, she can hold it at bay. She can stop time, and float, weightless, in a little pocket of space where no words are necessary. Where they are waiting for their son to be returned to them, and there is no time, so Wolfie is suspended too: he is not afraid, he is not alone. He is almost suspended with them, in this silent little place.

The stupidity of it.

Her family is all she can think about. The three of them, together.

God, even Charlie, if she must. Even the four of them. The four of them, together, is perfection compared to this.

It might be lost. It might be finished.

And it's all my fault.

In this space, in the eternity of it, it seems pointless to go on.

She struggles to keep her footing firmly in reality. She can't actually remember what she was thinking; why she did the things she did.

Charlie was hard to like, sure. *But was it worth losing her family over?*

All the things she had thought about Nick seem ludicrous, now. Huddled on the couch with her, he is exactly who she needs and the only comfort she can find in anything. She wants to hold on to him tightly, almost desperately: no one else understands this pain, this loss. On top of that, all her worries seem so trivial, now. *How much did it really matter that he disagreed with her on how much pocket money to give Charlie? How much did it really matter that he didn't jump every time Wolfie wanted something from him?*

In the tinny, hollow little corner of their new world, Olivia can see more clearly her own shortcomings. How much time she gave to Wolfie, and how little she gave to Nick. How obsessed she had become with the minute tasks of every day.

Is the floor clean?!

Is the dinner prepped?!

How agitated and harsh she was if Nick didn't do things exactly the way she wanted them done. When she should have been attending to the bigger picture of love and kindness and family time.

Now, these things seem small-minded and stupid. Like she has been living with blinkers on, more worried about whether Nick bought the right sort of apples than whether Wolfie felt loved. She can't even understand how tightly she has backed herself into a sad, cold, lonely little corner. When it's Nick here, on the couch with her. Nick feeling everything she is feeling.

Nick who is the only other person in the world who would give anything—*anything*—to have their son back.

Suddenly, the weird, floating sensation is unbearable to her. The untethered waiting. The limp, hapless sense of being suspended outside of time, waiting for Wolfie. She needs something to ground her. To bring her back to reality. To make amends, to set things right.

She sits up suddenly, looks down at Nick. Her shoulders are rigid; she doesn't know if she can undo what she has done. She is frightened by the choices she has made, the places she's been inside her mind.

Was Charlie that bad?

Was Nick?

She needs to start fixing it. She needs to know if she can.

She looks her husband straight in the eye and takes a deep breath.

"Bing won't be any good at step-parenting, either, you know," she says.

42

APRIL 1988

Far away from his family, Abby Shorten sits at a wooden desk in a room with fifteen or so other boys.

There are no girls, and the room is stuffy and dim. One window hangs slightly off its hinges, and dense spiderwebs populate the space on both sides of the flywire which loosely covers the gap.

The classroom sits alongside a major road. Trucks groan and shriek alongside the boys all day. The fan above them is broken, and whirs at a fraction of the pace that would be useful to move the stuffy air away from them and out the door. On each rotation, it clunks rhythmically: not only failing to cool the boys down, but relentlessly fanning the flames of their sensory distress.

Two teachers' aides flank the room. They are young and nervous. On the weekends, they scan the classifieds for an easier job.

Abby stares blankly at the sheet of paper in front of him. He couldn't hear what the teacher has told them to do over the biting invasion of all the other noises. The boy to his right—

Jonathan, only ten years old—taps his pencil on his desk, on and on and on. Marley, at the front of the room, has started wailing. The teacher walks in front of his desk and raps it hard with his fist.

"Quiet!" he barks. "Everyone needs to finish their writing in the next ten minutes!"

The teacher doesn't know it, but Abby can't read. Letters jumble themselves in front of his eyes, dancing and turning, laughing at his confusion. At his old school, Abby would tell the teachers that he couldn't work the letters out, but they hurried and pushed, not listening to him. They told him he didn't try hard enough; that if he spent more time concentrating, and less time disrupting the class, he'd be at the same level as his peers.

Now, his tiny world is made up of instructions, demands, impossible tasks.

Do it!

Read it!

Write it!

Be quiet!

Stop tapping!

Stop crying!

It's prep level, what's wrong with you!

It was bad enough when he was the only one falling behind, tapping, shouting, crying. Now he's in a room full of boys not coping.

In the evenings, they snatch five minutes here and there to talk, uninterrupted. Unsupervised. Marley tells Abby about aeroplanes in more detail than Abby cares for—but alone, Marley's voice running over him like gentle, warbling water, Abby feels calm. He rocks rhythmically and listens. He soothes himself. By morning, he has found some equilibrium.

Then it's back to the classroom. Where disequilibrium reigns.

43

TUESDAY, *Week Two*

Nick sits up slowly.

His eyes try to focus on Olivia, but she can see the questions, the confusion clouding them as he tries to ascertain what she knows, and what he should say.

He had been lying on the couch, lost in his new reality. He had even been thinking about talking to Olivia about it. How it had all gone so wrong.

Ever since Hannah asked him to move in with her, Nick had been panicking. He found it hard to say no to Hannah, but her expectations had thrown him completely. He had expected that their affair would fizzle out, and they would both keep it secret from Olivia forever, and he would live happily ever after with his beautiful wife and beautiful children.

Hannah did not strike him as the type of person who would enjoy a long-term relationship, or step-parenting, at all.

So her request, and the subsequent pressure she has been putting on him—even while his child is missing, for God's sake —had been so incongruous with his reality and expectations that he had just tried to avoid it as best he could.

But lying on the couch with Olivia, his mind had been spinning ever faster, trying to work it all out.

He can't shove this problem deep down inside like all the others. It is erupting into the world, with or without him. He can't hide it away.

How has he been so emotionally lazy, so emotionally blind?

And just as he's trying to work it out, explain it to himself for the first time—what changed when Wolfie was born, why he always has to be so nice—Olivia blindsides him.

He can't quite put it all together.

He remembers Patricia rubbing her protruding belly thoughtfully.

He remembers being in tears.

"Oh, Nick," she had said, her voice full of pity. "You didn't really believe I'd choose you, did you?"

He'd been too stunned by the revelation that Patricia was leaving him to dispute the logic of this statement. *If you date someone, and move in with them, and decide to have a child with them, haven't you already chosen them?*

Nevertheless, two weeks before their son was due to arrive in the world, Nick had come home to a half-empty flat. Patricia had already had removalists go through the house and take the things she wanted. She herself was on her way out the door— Nick was only getting this explanation in person because he'd felt unwell, and had left work early.

One picture hangs in his mind, suspended: Patricia, taking the handle of her cheerful little red suitcase, tipping it onto its side to wheel it out the door. Efficient. Bright. She had no intention of talking further about it; she did not care whatsoever about how Nick felt or what state she was leaving him in. She had paused in the doorway, one manicured hand on the door handle, though. As though this wasn't quite enough pain to leave Nick with. As though she wanted to kick him just a little bit more.

"I just wanted a baby," she'd said. "I never really wanted you."

And his world had fallen apart and never quite got put back together, ever again.

Now, Nick watches Olivia through bleary, exhausted eyes.

"What do you mean?" he asks, slowly, one painful item over another pressing relentlessly down on him, squeezing the air out of him, making his thoughts slow, strained.

"She told me she's thinking of taking on a stepchild," Olivia replies. She looks disinterested, not angry. "I'm assuming she means Charlie. And Wolfie." Here, Olivia's voice catches, and she looks away from Nick, the pain of Wolfie breaking her more than the pain of infidelity has done. She stares out their lounge room window, her vision impaired with tears.

Nick can't differentiate between her pain, though. She looks sad and defeated. His heart thuds dully in his chest.

He sees what he has done to her as a physical thing—that any pain she feels, her defeat, how crushed and empty she looks—that *he* has done it. He has put that brick on her chest. He has ripped the color out of her body.

"I'd like you to stop seeing her," Olivia goes on, still not looking at Nick, who is scrabbling to keep up. This emptiness is worse than anything he could imagine. He would have expected rage, hurt, tears, an eviction notice—and somehow, they might have been better.

More alive.

At the same time, and for a terrible moment, he feels grateful that Wolfie is missing—the outcome of this conversation he is certain would be something else entirely if Olivia had not been whitewashed by the last nine days. Immediately though, this thought fills him with shame.

He can't bear how empty and hollow she seems.

What a caricature of a partner he has become.

Olivia, his one true love, colorful above all the others. A kaleidoscope of astonishing things.

He feels suspended above himself: none of this feels real.

"I'm so sorry—" he starts, but Olivia waves a hand in front of her face, brushing everything behind his words away. She does not care.

"We can both do better," is all she says. "When Wolfie is back."

For a moment, he clings gratefully to the "we" in the sentiment—that they can work on this together. That Olivia wants to work on it too. That she's not even blaming him, entirely.

Nick puts his head in his heads and starts quietly to cry. "I'm so sorry," he mumbles, again, fingers pressing into his eyeballs, as though he might be able to stop not just the tears but the pain, the reality of it all. It all seems so completely senseless in this moment. All he ever wanted was his family. *How did he mess it all up so much?*

Olivia puts a hand tentatively on his shoulder. It's not exactly a warm gesture, but it's more than he would have expected in this moment. And it's fitting, somehow. It's a ginger movement, awkward, but an attempt at kindness, at saying, "we're on the same team," "we can help each other" and it makes Nick cry even harder. They sit like that, for a while.

Eventually, Nick reaches for a tissue, blows his nose. He looks at Olivia through messy red eyes.

"Olivia," he says. "There's something I didn't tell you about Patricia."

And saying it aloud—how ashamed, how unlovable, how foolish he had felt—somehow feels less like admitting his shortcomings and more like long-overdue relief.

It's not until much, much later that Nick finally remembers

the thought that has been eluding him, the tiny but significant thing that is not quite right: that his wife would never, ever, ever forget a detail like how much money was left to their child.

She wouldn't forget what she gave Wolfie for lunch last week. Her mind is a steel trap of information filed and stored with impeccable precision. He has drawn on the impressive abilities of her memory for over a decade.

There was no chance whatsoever she would forget about—and thus fail to tell him about—two hundred thousand dollars.

44

———

APRIL *1988*

Marley is in seclusion.

Abby dreads seclusion. It is a hot, dark little room at the end of the corridor. It's quieter there, but the darkness and the solitude presses down on him so fully that he feels like he is suffocating.

He is having difficulty thinking about Marley. He feels hot, his T-shirt clinging to him. He knows Marley will be screaming, but he can't hear him from where he is. He wants Marley to be okay. He wants to help him. It's not fair that Marley was taken away. Abby understands. It's the noise, and the heat, and the tasks, all the tasks that they can't keep up with, they can't filter and follow all the instructions.

Marley was just tapping. Just tapping his pencil. The noise was pushing Abby over the edge too, but he knows it was helping Marley. Marley was tapping to cope. He wasn't tapping to disrupt them. He wasn't being naughty, like the teacher thought he was.

He wants to explain. He wants to tell the teacher. Marley is only eleven. Abby is only two years older than Marley, but he feels responsible, he wants to look after him. He wants to look after all the younger boys. He's so big. He's older, and they all turn hopeful eyes toward him like he can make it better, like he can be their spokesperson, like he can represent them. He wants to hold it together so badly and not let them down.

But the teacher is talking. The fan is clunking. The trucks are screeching and honking. And it's so hot. So hot in this room.

A familiar vibration begins in his bones. There is a weird sensation, like his skull is too small for his brain, and his brain needs to get out, to escape. He starts rubbing at his arms. They feel tight, they feel too big, they feel too small. The roaring starts in his ears, and the teacher is in front of him, his mouth opening, words coming out, but Abby can only hear the roaring now. The other noises have morphed into stabbings, physical pain shooting into his head, his torso. He feels like he is being sucked into a vacuum, a screaming, swirling vortex of light and noise and stabbing and nothingness.

He doesn't know it, but he is screaming too, pounding his head against his desk, his arms jerking. Saliva runs down his chin. He needs it all to *stop*.

He just needs all the noise and all the violent, painful intrusions to his brain to stop.

IN ANOTHER WORLD, far, far away from Abby's one, their teacher, Brent, shouts for assistance. The teacher's aides come running.

They see Abby shouting and banging; they see him refusing to stop. The other boys start to wail and rock.

The teachers need Abby to *stop*. He is setting off the other boys. He's *disrupting* things. All three of them warn him. They shout and yell that he needs to stop it *right this minute*. They put their faces very close to his and try to look into his eyes, they shout closer to him, right in his face, so that he can hear them over all the noise. They shout in his face.

They see him refusing to listen.

They don't see his wild eyes, his panic, his complete loss of control. They just see his failure to cooperate.

They see a very big boy, refusing to do as he is told.

They're panicked and unprepared, they just need him to stop. But they're a little bit angry too. They're angry that he won't listen; they're angry that they're in this job and nobody told them it would be like this, nobody told them what it was really like. "Prone restraint" was just a theory, an absolutely last resort solution.

Nobody told them they'd be doing it every week.

Nobody told them how bad it would feel: this mixture of uncertainty, anger, fear, and lack of training.

They're pulling him from his chair.

For his own safety, they will tell police, later.

Tom, the youngest aide, kneels on Abby's back, his knees pressing into his shoulder blades.

Kieran straddles his legs.

Abby continues to bang his head into the floor, and Brent presses a knee into the back of his head.

Just to stop him from hurting himself.

Abby pees himself, and vomits, but they have to keep him safe, they have to stop him banging his head, so they hold him just a bit longer.

Just a little bit more.

45

―――――――

DISAPPEARANCE DAY – *Monday, Week One*

Olivia stares at her face in the mirror.

She takes deep breaths, watching the lines around her mouth, willing them to smooth out to something calmer, something prettier.

Wolfie is on the trampoline, and she should go to him. She should apologize for screaming. She should explain that she's just tired; that she shouldn't shout at him like that.

That she loves him.

That she wants to spend time with him.

But she's not feeling those things, not yet. The familiar guilt creeps in, clouding her eyes. She watches her frown deepening, the lines on her face becoming more pronounced. The little turn at the corners of her mouth resettling into something angry. Spiteful, even.

She wishes Wolfie would come back inside. That he would apologize for not helping her. That he'd pack up his trucks, quietly and efficiently, and trot over to the kitchen bench, eager to help. That they would stir batter and cut cookies together like Olivia had imagined they would this morning, when she was helping him pick out his clothes.

Like she had imagined they would as her stomach swelled and changed with the bulk of him, growing inside her.

She had imagined so many possibilities.

Olivia stares at herself in the mirror. Minutes tick by, and she can see the conflict working across her face.

The desire to go to Wolfie, and repair things.

The desire to leave him there, and punish him.

To wait for him to feel bad for not helping her, and come back to her, contrite.

She stares in the mirror, stares and stares, being pulled one way, and then another.

She's so tired.

Her eyelids start to droop.

The turmoil inside her makes her want to lie down. Just close her eyes. Just for a few minutes.

Perhaps she could rest, and Wolfie could think about his behavior.

Just for a few more minutes.

Just enough to feel her absence and want to make it right with her.

Olivia blinks in the mirror.

The house is completely silent.

Beyond the house is completely silent too.

Olivia feels the pull of her bed. It's just a few short steps away. *What would be the harm?*

Wolfie was on the trampoline. He wouldn't talk to strangers —he was far too nervous. Once upon a time, perhaps, but not now. Now there was no chance of him being lured into a stranger's car with kindnesses or lollies.

She kicks off her shoes and slips under her doona, the bamboo sheets caressing her skin, her head sinking into her pillow with so much relief it seemed a miracle she'd been able to keep herself upright all morning at all.

She closes her eyes.

She rests for a minute.

She thinks she really must get up and go to Wolfie. But she's so tired.

Her bed is so comfortable.

Just a few more minutes.

Just a little bit more.

46

When the call comes, *Olivia knows.*

There is wailing, and rushing, and hushed voices.

Olivia and Bing are bundled through the next-door neighbor's front door, whispered thanks, no explanations. And Olivia's mother and father tear off in the old, rusted, noisy station wagon with barely a word.

Margie from next door is soft and terrified. She speaks in whispers, turns the television on, gives Bing and Olivia ice cream on the couch. Olivia sees tears in her eyes. She is older than Amelia: her kids have already left home. She has a tight perm and soft folds of skin above the waist of her jeans, and Olivia wants to burrow her head in her bosom and sob and sob and sob.

No one has told her anything yet, but they don't have to. Olivia already knows.

Something's happened to Abby.

47

———

Disappearance Day

"Hello, Wolfie."

The man had been sitting in his car over the road.

He had not intended to talk to the child, he really hadn't.

He had seen him here before.

Well, that was not true. That made it sound like an accident; that he had just happened upon him on this street, a mere coincidence. If he was really honest, he had come here to watch before. He had sat in this very street, shaded by a youthful plain tree, his window open just enough to hear snatches of conversations.

Wolfie with his mother, examining something in the garden. Asking about where the beetles lived, or how the bird died.

He'd watched Olivia, with the hard set of her mouth, the stiff way she held her shoulders when she was angry.

He couldn't really say why he kept coming back. He had told himself that this was the last time.

But then the child had emerged, scuffing his shoes, kicking idly at rocks on the path down the side of the house.

He'd watched him for a while, waiting for Olivia to trail behind him, pointing things out to him patiently, or telling him what to do or what she wanted, her voice hard—he could tell from the first moment of seeing her which it would be that day. Soft Olivia, or hard Olivia.

Wolfie looked forlorn. His path was aimless. He wasn't making a beeline for anything. He kicked stones and plucked leaves, wandering closer and closer to the front gate. His lips were moving, but the man could not hear any words.

Wolfie stopped beside a camellia tree, idly pulling petals off a bright red flower. He paused midway through to wipe at his eyes, and the man squinted, trying to see better.

Was Wolfie crying?

The man scanned the front yard and the wedge of back garden he could see. There was no sign of Olivia.

He wound his window down a little bit more and listened carefully.

It was one of those beautiful summer days where everything was perfectly still. The sky was blue from horizon to horizon. A faint hum—bees, or distant traffic?—did nothing to disturb the peacefulness of it. The sheer expanse of sky and the perfect temperature made the man's heart soar.

The beauty of this day.

The stretching, empty, lovely solitude.

And this lovely boy, all alone.

The man inched forward until he was level with Wolfie's driveway.

Wolfie didn't notice him. He was staring down at some red petals in his hand, his face blank, his eyes seeing something far, far away.

The man wound his window down completely and rested his arm along the length it. He hesitated for a moment. And then:

"Hello, Wolfie," he said.
Inexplicably, the boy smiled.

48

TUESDAY, *Week Two*

Olivia is watching Nick quietly.

She's trying to make sense of everything he told her. She doesn't think even Nick understands it. But it's something. A starting point.

"Why did you never tell me?" she'd asked, bewildered. She knew Patricia wasn't great, but she had no idea how bizarrely their relationship had ended.

"I think I was ashamed. That someone I trusted...I misjudged so terribly. Like, I didn't even notice she didn't love me. What kind of an idiot doesn't notice such a thing?"

Nick looks down, his features twisting into something unfamiliar. Bitterness, Olivia thinks.

"So...what happened?"

"I got over it. I fought for contact with Charlie. I don't think she expected that. I think in her weird little world, where people were disposable, it hadn't even occurred to her that I might be invested in having a relationship with my child. She tried to throw money at the problem, but I think even her parents were on my side. They wouldn't give her money to keep pushing it through the courts. She eventually agreed to shared care. She hated it, though. It wasn't quite what she had in mind."

Nick pauses for a while. "I don't think I ever really processed it, though. I thought I had dealt with it, moved on, forgiven myself. But then Wolfie came along. And all your time suddenly shifted to doing things for Wolfie. With Wolfie. And I think deep down I was terrified that you were choosing your kid over me, too. It made me question whether I was really loved. But instead of dealing with that, I tried to hide it, too. I just tried to be a good dad, a good husband, accommodate everyone else's needs. Because I think I was really scared that if I made too much noise, asserted what I wanted, that I wouldn't be worth it anymore."

Olivia looks thoughtful. "But you did assert yourself," she says. "Especially with Charlie. About how to parent him."

Nick thinks about this for a while. "Did I, really, though?" he says, eventually. "I think I was just fighting for a corner where I had some clout. I felt like I didn't get to make any choices, about Wolfie, about us. I felt like you just took the reins after Wolfie was born. I just had to go along for the ride. And I know it's a copout. I know that. But maybe if I felt like you had all the power, parenting Charlie was one little corner of the world where I got to have more say. I'm not saying I was right. I'm just saying I can see how it happened. It was lazy and selfish, sure. But if I'm honest, I can see how I ended up there. I think I resented you for the hoops that I was making *myself* jump through. So I was trying to control something. However small or petty."

Olivia looks doubtful. For a moment, she looks like she is going to say something, but Nick goes on:

"It was eating away at me, and I didn't even know it. If you're always thinking about other people and you don't believe they're also thinking about you. So when Hannah hit on me, I felt like I deserved to be wanted. I deserved to have some fun. I felt like no one else seemed to care, why should I be the only one caring? Why should I be the only one working so hard to look out for everyone else's needs? Why shouldn't I be selfish? It sounds so stupid. And of course, I wasn't really looking out for your needs. I was second-guessing them. And now that I'm saying it, it seems so obvious that I could have just talked to you about it. Told you how I felt, what I was scared of. But I really thought it might be the same. That I wasn't good enough. That I was superfluous. That—" Here Nick chokes up, the sentiment —finally acknowledged—overwhelming him.

"That Wolfie was who you really wanted, not me."

Olivia hesitates. It all feels like too much. Wolfie is gone. Nick is crying on their couch. She feels overloaded, unable to compute everything Nick is saying. She really just wants to put it aside and deal with it later. *But isn't that exactly what he's telling her? That he feels like he comes last?*

She reaches out, tentatively, and puts her hand over Nick's. Lets him cry for a while.

Is this where it all went wrong?

Is talking about it how they can make it right?

Finally, Nick looks up. "I think what I really wanted was a better connection with you. But it didn't seem possible. So I opted for any connection. And I should have come to you. I should have told you how I felt. But I didn't want to ask questions because I was scared of what the answer might be. But that's no excuse. Because the answers would have freed us both. I wanted to avoid how bad it felt, but all I've done is make the pain much worse."

Olivia hesitates. She's still not sure. She squeezes his hand and squeezes her eyes shut.

LATER, Nick is showing Charlie patiently how to improve on his coffee-making. He looks haggard and old. But there is something compelling in his actions. He shows Charlie how to level the coffee grounds, how tight to pack them. How to adjust the grinder if he wants the coffee to pour differently. He smiles at Charlie sadly and squeezes his shoulder, somehow encapsulating both his love for his child and his regret that he can't do better in that moment. In the moment where their child is missing and their hope is seeping away from them like blood.

Something shifts inside Olivia.

She knows perhaps it's her grief, her emptiness. But it feels like seeing the same old thing anew. With fresh eyes, or clearer eyes, perhaps. Eyes stripped away of all the things that matter less.

Even battered by life, even in great pain himself, Nick is trying to look after them. He is watching her and Charlie, wondering what they need from him. Trying to hold the fort, and keep them all afloat, or whatever metaphor Olivia is stretching for. The one that equals goodness, and kindness, and helping. Of holding them all up.

Even as he reckons with the flaws inside himself. Even, perhaps, if it's the flaws that motivate him.

He has made mistakes, sure. There's Bing, for a start. But if Nick made a mistake there, Olivia did, too. *And one could argue that Olivia's error was the more calculated, the more concerning.*

The more unforgivable one.

Now, her heart lurches in her chest. An orchestrated affair. Keeping secret a strange inheritance. Somewhere deep inside, Olivia knows whose transgressions are the more deplorable. *Any sane partner would leave you for things like that, wouldn't they?*

She yearns toward the idea of starting again, being better, doing better. She wants to tell Nick how crazy things got.

She got.

How crazy she got.

She wants his forgiveness and reassurance that they're okay.

That she's okay.

But she watches him trying to help Charlie, she feels him trying to support her, and she vows instead she will just do better. She will make it up to him. She can't tell him, or they will truly break. Forever.

"Would you like a coffee, Olivia?"

Charlie's question startles her. She can see the uncertainty on his face, the eagerness. For the hundredth time, she wonders if she imagined it all. He looks like he is longing for her to say yes, and to enjoy his coffee, and approve of him.

She feels like she is coming up from under water, from murkiness, from not being able to breathe.

She smiles gently at Charlie.

"That's very kind of you, thank you, Charlie," she says. Her eyes flick to Nick's, and there's something there that stops her heart. It's gratitude, that she's trying, too.

Gratitude and hopefulness.

That their future could look a little different.

That if Wolfie is just returned to them, if he is found and fine and back where he belongs, if the world is pieced back together again, then they might all work hard enough to make it okay.

49

TUESDAY, *Week Two*

Detective Rolands hangs up the phone slowly.

Her Sydney colleague had been surprised.

"I've spoken to the sister, too. Neither of them mentioned a brother," Rolands had said. She had just wanted someone to go speak to the parents. She'd had a chat to them over the phone, but felt like someone in person might get them talking more.

She didn't have any particular questions. They were elderly, and supportive, by all accounts. But you talk to everyone you can lay your hands on in a missing child investigation. Maybe they'd remember something, some little fact that seemed irrelevant but wasn't.

And it was just the merest happenstance that Detective Rose knew who they were.

"Uh, I met them," she had said, wracking her brain for the context. "I was on the front desk, just helping out over lunch. Let me see." She tapped away at her computer, the phone jammed against her ear.

"Missing child. Nineteen eighty-eight," she'd said, triumphant. "He ran away from a special school in Sydney.

Another child died, a student. Abby disappeared immediately afterwards. There was a big search, but he was presumed dead. The school had stated he wouldn't survive on his own. Said he was a bit simple. Got a whole lot of terrible press. No charges were ever laid. The kid who died had been held down by staff because he was violent, or something, and then a whole heap of parents came forward with complaints about how their kids were treated. Most of them had been restrained in similar ways for minor things, like their stims, tapping or flapping and stuff. The school was shut down. I didn't get a lot of the details. They come in most years, apparently."

Rose tapped away some more.

"We found an Adam with the right birth date at an address in Melbourne. Short, not Shorten, though. Adam Short. Mixed up with some guy who was in and out of juvie, a handful of minor offences as an adult. Shoplifting, that kind of thing. But of course, just a first name and a DOB, it was a long shot. I said we'd send an officer round and see if it was the right kid. He's an adult now, of course. Forty-four, forty-five. I told them if it was the right guy we'd give him their details if he wanted to make contact, but that I couldn't do any more.

"Anyway, wrong guy. Or at least, he denied any knowledge of them. Gave the officer pretty short shrift, apparently. I did give the parents a follow-up call, and they've been calling me ever since. Wanting us to go again. Wanting to send letters. Wanting the address to go and see for themselves. Wanting to know why charges were never laid against the teachers involved. Wanting contact with the family of the kid who died. They seemed a bit of a mess, to be honest. The school isn't even in operation anymore. I doubt anyone can remember anything with enough certainty to be useful."

But Rolands was no longer even listening.

Two missing kids, in the one family?

"Give me that address. I might just go and have a chat to

this Adam," she'd said, already standing, already swiping her keys off the bench.

As she drives, she curses Olivia. *Why wouldn't she mention a missing brother?* Rolands can't work out how the two missing boys might fit together, but it's certainly bloody odd enough to look at further. *Why would Olivia keep that from her?*

Dog-legging through suburban Melbourne, she wonders about the Shorten/Hitchens family. It wasn't that they were more disconnected or more broken than any of the other families she came across in her line of work.

It's just that they didn't seem to know it.

50

Daniel Shorten closes *the door behind the police officers harder than he intended to.*

Amelia is on the couch, unmoving, and Olivia and Bing creep out from wherever they were loitering and slink around her like stray cats—wary and hopeful. They've overheard enough. Still, Olivia wants to be sure.

"What does 'scaling back' mean?" she asks her mother. Amelia doesn't answer.

Olivia waits for a while, then narrows her eyes, her face becoming harder. Her little chin juts out, somewhere between defiant and resolute. "We'll look for him. We'll look for him every day, for the rest of our lives, and never stop until we find him," she declares, watching her mother closely.

Olivia is very careful not to say any more. Not "Why did you send him to that horrible place?" or "Why did you force him to leave us?" and certainly not "If you had kept him at home, none of this would have happened!" She is only nine, but already she knows that while all of those things are valid, saying them aloud might break her mother.

It takes her a long, long time to realize that her mother is already broken, no matter what she does or doesn't say.

WHEN DANIEL DECLARES *they are moving to Sydney later that year, Abby starts to be erased.*

There is no bedroom for him in the new house.

If his belongings remain, Olivia never sees them again. Once, crying, she shouts at Daniel, "We don't even have any pictures of him! It's like you want him to be gone!" and the back of Daniel's hand across her face is an explosion, a revelation—Olivia comes to understand that silence does not mean nothing. That silence, in fact, might harbor more pain than a person has the resources to cope with. And if it's not pain, then what is her father so angry about?

Even Bing, with whom she tries desperately to keep Abby alive with, to honor him, to not forget—even Bing seems just fine without her brother. Approaching high school, her attention is taken up by boys and makeup and styling her hair. "Don't you ever think about him?" she asks Bing once, and Bing tosses her hair—dyed red, for the first time—and says, "If he hadn't been so difficult, none of this would have happened. He should have had better self-control." Bing snaps her compact mirror closed with an air of finality, and her eyes meet Olivia's. "You'd be better off looking forward, not backward," she tells her, and for a moment Olivia aches towards something deep and careful in Bing's eyes, but it's gone as soon as Olivia registers it, Bing's eyes sliding away from her, her face going blank.

Olivia thinks she hears Daniel in her words, but maybe she just hears coping.

Amelia doesn't comment on the red hair, or the makeup, and Olivia wonders where Bing gets the money to pay for these things. Once, Bing doesn't come home from school until after midnight, and Olivia pesters Amelia all night, every hour, her panic consuming her.

Amelia is indifferent, unreachable. "She'll be fine; she'll be home soon."

To Olivia, everything is exaggerated, a million feelings and fears fitting onto a pin head, everything connected to everything else. But the rest of her family seem to tilt in the opposite direction—everything stretched far, far apart, disconnected.

She struggles to remember Abby, and they struggle to forget.

51

———

TUESDAY, *Week Two*

Olivia huddles in her en suite and calls Paul's offices.

Furtive, she thinks to herself.

After barely being able to get out of bed for days, there is enough panic to drive her into action. Now, she has some purpose—a family to hold together. If only Wolfie would come back.

She's always been able to achieve things against monumental odds.

Paul is very busy, but she knows he will take her call.

This is the way they have always worked. High-school sweethearts, Olivia knows she takes advantage a little bit. But Paul never seems to mind.

"Don't lodge anything," she tells him. "Destroy it all."

After she hangs up, she has a flash of doubt. *Is she making the right decision?* The uncertainty weighs on her.

Secrets. Misunderstandings.

Charlie, mostly. Charlie in her life, in her personal space, forever.

Except—it's not forever. It's just for three more years.

Long days, fast years.

Is it the disequilibrium of Wolfie being missing? she wonders. *Is she clinging onto something comforting and known in a period of weakness, of despair?*

Is she throwing away her one chance at a peaceful life in the country, away from Nick and Charlie and anxiety and the daily grind of work-parent-life-admin-bed?

But her mind has not always been her friend.

She lets her heart pull her along, for a change.

She finds Nick exactly where she left him.

She crawls back alongside him on the couch.

She burrows under his arm.

She wonders, if they can just find Wolfie, and if she never tells him what she has done, if she can live with the half-truths left between them.

Three long years.

"Nick," she says, her voice urgent, breathless. "When Wolfie's back, I want us to find a therapist. I want to talk about us, and Patricia. And Charlie. I need you to be able to talk about the things that worry me about Charlie. I need a professional to help me, to help us. To move forward."

She waits for Nick to answer, and holds her breath.

52

———

TUESDAY, Week Two

Abby looks apologetically at his partner, who is gaping at him, his face etched with shock and fear.

"I didn't mean to. I mean. It just happened."

A pause.

"I mean, he wanted to come. It was like he knew me."

Ray continues to stare at Abby, a wild look in his eyes.

They're standing in the kitchen of their shabby one-bedroom apartment. Wolfie is playing with some toy cars which Abby had procured a few days before.

Usually, Abby works in the local library filing books three days a week. He still can't read with ease, and he is laboriously slow. But he was placed there through employment services, with additional supports.

This week, he has called in sick every day.

Ray doesn't match the stereotype of a truckie—he is small, and quiet, and thoughtful. Today, though, he is frightened, and fear can breed anger. Abby squirms in front of him, turning this way and that.

"Haven't you seen the news?" Ray asks, his voice faint. He

leans against the kitchen counter and stares at Wolfie. His eyes cross back to Abby, who looks panicked and pale.

"I wasn't sure what to do," he says. He looks like a frightened rabbit, terrified that Ray will yell at him, or—even if Ray's perfectly silent about it—be angry with him nevertheless.

Abby's vulnerable innocence softens Ray's anger—which isn't even really anger. Just panic, too, that everything they have worked so hard for—this flat, their anonymous, under-the-radar life—could be snatched from them at any moment. Though Abby miraculously managed to stay out of trouble his entire life, Ray was in and out of the justice system for most of his, even with Johnny taking him under his wing and trying to guide him in the right direction.

Sometimes Ray wonders what his life would have been like if Johnny had been his dad, from his very first day.

It never helps to think like that, though.

Things only really turned around for Ray when he met Abby. Just like Ray himself a few years before, Abby had arrived under their bridge, and crumpled against the wall. Ray had immediately started to rise, to go to him, but Johnny touched his arm, and Ray had sat back down.

They'd watched Abby quietly for a while. Johnny was kind, but he was also cautious.

Eventually, he'd nodded at Ray, and Ray had made his way over to where Abby lay, half against the wall, his breathing still erratic, his eyes closed. Ray had been frightened momentarily, but when he spoke to Abby, softly, Abby's eyes had flown open, his terror so immediate and so enormous that Ray had stepped backward without thinking.

Instinctively, he knew how to soothe Abby, without ever having exchanged a word with him. He showed him his hands, palms upward, trying to say, "You're safe here, you're safe with me." And he'd gone a decent distance away and sat down, his eyes down. "We'll help you, if you like," he'd said, and Abby had cried, and cried, and cried, and Ray didn't need to ask him any questions, because he knew that moment, under the bridge, when you were all alone and your life had changed so ferociously there weren't even any words to say.

For the first time in his life Ray had a role, even if Abby might have disagreed with it.

"You said you didn't want to talk to them." Ray is watching Abby closely. His mind is whirring. Abby calls him at 10 p.m. every day when he is away, but Ray had called him too, this trip. Every time he stopped for a break he called, just to check. Ever since that police officer had knocked on their door.

Abby had spiralled into panic that day. Ray hadn't seen him so distressed for years. And it wasn't that he didn't want to see his parents—just that he had put them in a box somewhere in his mind, and left them there for thirty years. And when they had finally gone into a homelessness service—together, spurring each other on—Abby had declared his family were all dead. The social worker had offered to try to find any remaining relatives, but Abby had been insistent.

There was no family.

There was only Ray.

Slowly, slowly, they had built up a life. Some emergency housing. A Centrelink account. Some job seeker support. Ray had already taught Abby the alphabet, but they found they could get more help. There were services that existed just to help them find a job. Their heads spun with the possibilities.

It was hard to trust people, after thirty-odd years on the streets or in the justice system.

It was hard to ask for help.

But they did. And three years later, Ray felt like they were finally okay.

Except now there was a small child in their living room.

A small child that half the nation was looking for.

Wolfie seemed happy enough. He was lining up his toy cars,

murmuring to himself. Occasionally, one car would be moved out of line, made to carefully execute an imagined task, and returned to its spot in the line-up.

Ray was panicking, but he was also mystified.

"Did you drive?" he asks, astonished.

"How did you find....?" His voice trails off.

"Doesn't he miss his family?" he whispers, and Wolfie looks up at him then, and Ray's heart skips a beat, because he looks just like Abby—the wide eyes, the high cheekbones. The peculiar little set to his chin.

Abby looks confused, and glances to Ray, to Wolfie, and back to Ray again. And suddenly Ray sees it.

"That's your sister on the news," he says slowly, pieces of the puzzle starting to make sense to him. Like, why on earth Abby —who never talks to anyone, who doesn't like people at all— would pluck a child off the street and take him home and think it was okay.

"Olivia," Ray murmurs, staring at Abby. "Olivia Shorten." They never talk about the details. Just once, they had told each other, holding on to each other in the dark. What happened to them.

Ray, watching his father hold his mother over that balcony, the savage satisfaction on his face as he let her look at her son one last time, then casually let go of her.

Abby, watching the teachers pressing down on Marley, the way his legs twitched, the urine seeping across the floor. The whole classroom in uproar: the noise of it. The panic.

"He can't breathe!" Abby had screamed, but no one listened to them, no one cared, they just wanted them all to be quiet, to comply. And Abby had watched Marley's eyes roll back, glaze over, the fight leach out of him and away, away, away.

"He's just having a holiday with Uncle Abby," Abby falters now, his frown deepening. "He was crying. He was all alone.

And he ran to me when I said hello, like he knew who I was. Like—"

But Ray interrupts him. "How did you find them?" His mind is working overtime. The police officer had told them Abby's parents were trying to find him. That they were seeking to press charges against the school—long since closed down—and teachers involved in the *incident*—here the police officer had looked at Abby gingerly—and explained that they had found an Adam with the right birth date, though his surname had changed. She had just thought she'd swing by and knock on the door.

Abby had been so distressed by this news. He had crawled under the table and rocked gently back and forth, making a low humming sound. Ray had carefully closed the blinds, turned off the television, treading lightly on the carpet. Then he went and sat under the table with Abby. Apart, but together.

Abby didn't need to say anything. Ray knows this story like he knows his own. He may have only heard the details once, but the story underneath it is as familiar as breathing. This is what made his partner tick.

They abandoned him.

They didn't want him.

They sent him to that awful school where his friend had died, and no one had even done anything. No one had even cared. And he had run, run, run, found somewhere dark, somewhere quiet, but it wasn't even very far, how long had he run for, was it five minutes, was it ten, was it twenty or thirty?

No one had come for him. No one had helped.

How hard was it to find a thirteen-year-old boy sleeping rough in the city?

Abby had said "wrong Adam" more firmly than Ray had ever seen him say anything in his life, and closed the door before the police officer could ask any more questions.

Abby didn't know it, but they had tried to find him. That the police that Ray and Johnny avoided were the same police searching known homeless hangouts for a boy matching his description. So in some ways, Johnny and Ray saved him; and in others, they did not.

After a couple of weeks, the search for Abby had been scaled back. Because how long could a small boy with Abby's "difficulties" survive by himself on the streets? The school reported he was low-functioning. The family insisted he could ask for help, he could tell someone his name, his address, that when he was calm he could function perfectly well, but the school advised they doubted that very much.

But now Ray waves a hand impatiently, waving away his last question, because it's not important right now. For all that Abby struggles with—with people, with noise, with functioning when those two things are combined together—it is clear that Wolfie has found some way to feel comfortable in their little home. More pressing: "Why didn't you call the police when you saw him on the news?"

Abby looks terrified again. And Ray knows the answer to that—the question is superfluous the moment it has left his mouth. He and Abby have spent enough time on the streets to know how they will be treated by law enforcement officers. And they might have a flat and steady jobs now, but mistrust is engrained in them. There's only so many times you can be treated as worthless without it expecting that it is the way it will be.

Ray gently takes Abby's hand.

"We have to call the police," he says. "We have to take him home."

But before Abby can answer, there is a loud knock on the door.

EPILOGUE

Two Months Later

Olivia is sitting on her back deck, sipping a glass of wine.

Wolfie is playing on the trampoline.

"I'm off," says Nick, poking his head through the back door. "I'll take your folks to their hotel to settle in before I bring them back here."

"I'll come with you," Charlie offers, and Nick reaches an arm out, half guiding Charlie with him, half just using it as an excuse to hold him close.

Olivia murmurs her understanding. Everyone is nervous. She doesn't even know if Abby and Ray will turn up. It's been hit and miss with just her little family, a forty-sixty strike rate that they'll come when they say they will. Bringing Amelia and Daniel into the mix will probably overwhelm them, and Olivia is trying not to be too hopeful.

Olivia pictures Abby and Ray at home, sitting quietly on their ragged red couch. It's worn through on the arms, the fawn threading underneath hanging in some places all the way down to the floor.

The first time she had seen it, she had felt... *something.* It wasn't distaste, and it wasn't pity. She still can't really pin down that day to any narrative that makes sense. It was a few days after Wolfie was home, the jagged edges of feelings she couldn't manage gradually feeling manageable. Wolfie had clung to her, those first few days. He was like a puzzle piece, clicking to her with finality and ease—but it wasn't fear or brokenness. It had seemed like relief and love.

There was the mess of the police processes, and the mess of how to move forward. But it had only taken a day—Olivia was certain she wanted to see Abby. She was confused, and frightened, but it wasn't anger. It was the pull toward wanting to understand, to connect, dogging her her whole life. Abby had taken her child and she couldn't make sense of it, and the only way forward was to see him, to hear him speak.

Besides that, he was her brother. She had yearned for him in some form her whole life.

Rolands had been frank. "I don't think he's a danger to you or Wolfie. I think he's had a hard life, and I think he's probably diagnosable with something. We're having him assessed as a priority. In the meantime, I don't think you should see him." She'd been cagey about where Abby had been all these years, who he lived with, what she thought he might be diagnosed with.

How they had found him, when no one else had managed to find him for thirty years.

Olivia couldn't make sense of any of it; she sat and cried.

Now, Olivia pictures them there, Ray drinking beer, Abby drinking water, facing the television that they rarely turn on. The image soothes her. Her breathing slows.

She won't mind if they don't turn up. They have the rest of their lives to have dinners together.

Whenever Abby is ready.

She feels a pang for Amelia though. It had taken all of Olivia's skills to discourage her from landing on Abby's doorstep the day that they found him. Rolands had been livid, for a start. Kind first, of course.

We have Wolfie.

He seems fine. We're bringing him to you now.

We'll have a doctor check him.

There are other fragments that Olivia can't remember clearly. Was it Rolands who organized the psych assessment for Wolfie? Were they looking for information about what had happened to him, or were they assessing the things Olivia had reported concerns with?

"Why didn't you tell me you had a missing brother?" Rolands had barked down the phone at her, later, or was it the same call? It has all merged together, dense and overwhelming.

He's okay, he's okay, he's okay.

Nick, running to her as she crumpled to the floor.

He's okay, he's okay, he's okay.

Was it then, or later, that she tried to talk about Abby? The next few hours went so slowly, and so fast.

There was Wolfie, quiet and wide-eyed, but running to her, his arms outstretched. Clinging to her so hard she thought they might be welded together forever, and she didn't mind at all.

There was Nick, sobbing and sobbing and sobbing, the weight of the last nine days crashing though him, tsunami-like, rushing in and rushing out in chaos, but leaving something calm behind.

Her family.

"Squish cuddle!" was the first thing that Wolfie said, calm as you like, as though it was any day, and nothing out of the ordinary had happened. And Nick had sobbed more, not able to lift him the way he usually did, to squash him in a cuddle between the two of them. He had crushed Wolfie to him, between them on the floor.

And Rolands, was she angry? Olivia is not even sure of that

now. She recalls not being able to answer that question: *Why didn't she mention her missing brother?*

"*We weren't allowed to talk about him*" sounds ludicrous, in retrospect, given her missing four-year-old, and given that she was conversing with police detectives, not her mother.

Now, she thinks about all the ways they buried Abby. Her mother, her father, Bing. *How did that happen?*

Was she really not allowed to talk about him, or did she just learn to stop asking questions because when she did, the heaviness was suffocating?

"*It hurt too much*" might have been more accurate, but Olivia was trying to process the world, and the ripples that had been ricocheting out ever since nineteen eighty-eight were too much to incorporate in her head, let alone out loud.

"How?" she'd asked Rolands, confused, dazed, and got the barest of explanations: "He found you in the phone book."

"Why?" was harder to answer, and not even on Olivia's radar at that point in time. She had been so desperate, so overwhelmed, so shattered, that she could not function beyond seeing Wolfie. The rest of it is a blur.

NOW AMELIA IS DESPERATE. So desperate that Abby will be terrified.

"It's been thirty years, Mum," Olivia had tried to explain to her. "He can barely stay with me for five minutes. He's believed we abandoned him for all this time. He's overwhelmed."

It had taken days to see him. All Rolands would offer was that he was being detained and was cooperating. Olivia tried to imagine her brother, in interviews, the questions and recriminations, and she couldn't picture him. It was a parallel world that she had never allowed herself to imagine—Abby, as an adult. Abby, doing adult things.

All she could see was the boy, with the big round face. How that boy would have responded to having a family again. To being at a police station.

Rolands called her every day.

He's seeing a social worker today.

He's seeing a psychiatrist today.

His intentions don't seem to be malicious.

And every time, Olivia asked, "When can I see him?"

On the third day, Rolands arranged it. Olivia had stepped through the doorway of the tiny flat. It was run-down, but neat and clean. Rolands opened the door for her, then moved quietly to sit on the decrepit red couch. Two men were standing as far away from the doorway as they could possibly get, and Olivia's heart lurches, because Abby is thin, and his face isn't round, and he looks just like Wolfie. And she had cried, and cried, and cried, and Abby had come to her, had stood next to her, and tentatively touched her arm. And—awkwardly, tenderly—tried to shush her tears away.

Amelia and Daniel have been down and back from Sydney numerous times. And every time Abby refuses to see them.

Rolands had advised that—after numerous specialist assessments, interviews with Ray and Abby—they would not press any charges, and passes on, with Abby's permission, that the psychologist suggested a formal assessment for Autism Spectrum Disorder. Wolfie is likewise awaiting assessment, and Olivia tries to explain it to her mother.

The possibility of a diagnosis for Wolfie is a relief, although Olivia struggles with guilt about not noticing. *Shouldn't she, out of all the mothers in the world, have seen what was happening?*

Her own counsellor reminds her that all presentations of autism are different, though. From what she remembers of

Abby, through the fallible memory of a child, he presented very differently to Wolfie. At least, Olivia cannot remember his anxiety. Only how he struggled with noise. How noise overwhelmed him to the point that he could not function at all.

How he couldn't quite understand the social mores of other boys.

"Does it matter?" asks Amelia, as Olivia tries to explain the process, what it means, and Olivia thinks about this for a little while.

"No," she says eventually. "Not really. Wolfie will get funding for some supports. I don't know if adults do." Here, she makes a mental note to look into this, if Abby wants her to. She'll mention it to Nick later, and he'll remember her foolproof memory, how she never needs to keep a list, she just keeps it all locked away inside that beautiful head of hers. He'll remember the two hundred thousand dollars. But he'll—carefully, consciously—put it to the side, to be brought up in family therapy at some point, if it seems important. They're going weekly, and the therapist had invited them to bring Charlie in to the next session.

To himself, he wonders if the money was an apology. *Maybe Patricia looked back on her cruelty, her calculatedness, and it was the only way she knew how to make amends?*

God knows, he understands how hard it is to look directly at your flaws yourself.

"But it might just help Abby *and* us to understand him a little better," Olivia goes on. "In the meantime, I can send you some resources if you like."

Personally, Olivia thinks that Amelia is going to need more than resources. She's googled some local therapists for her mother. She knows what six months' worth of guilt feels like. She can't begin to imagine thirty-one years of it. Not that she can imagine either of her parents agreeing to therapy.

Then again, she never imagined they went to the police

year in, year out, keeping Abby on a missing persons radar, in the only way they knew how. She knows that last visit was the link that led Rolands to Wolfie. She knows Ray would have helped Abby bring Wolfie back to her anyway, but she is grateful nevertheless.

Maybe she doesn't know her parents as well as she thought she did.

Now, though, she turns her attention to dinner.

"I'm going to make burritos, Little One," she calls to Wolfie. "You wanna help?"

Wolfie shades his eyes to look his mother, then shakes his head, his lips moving, fingers counting. Olivia feels afraid, but also determined. She has a stack of books on her bedside table. Help is available, and she will use it.

"Uncle Abby and Uncle Ray are coming," she reminds him, watching him carefully. But all she sees is a brief, small smile on his little face, then he returns to murmuring to himself.

Olivia still hasn't quite got her head around Wolfie and Abby. When Abby first visited them—and Olivia had been careful to visit him, alone, several times first, before extending the invitation to her home—Wolfie had trotted up to Abby and handed him a truck, then sat at his feet without a word. And just as Wolfie had expected him to, Abby sat down with him, moving his truck into a position that appeared to satisfy Wolfie immensely.

Silently, they'd moved their vehicles about, Wolfie nodding occasionally and smiling contentedly to himself. "Vroom, vroom," he'd said softly, every now and then.

Olivia had watched on in wonder. Ray had seemed uncertain, apologizing for Abby in a roundabout way, more conscious of the social norms that Abby might be breaching: "He might stay there a while." But Olivia had waved his concerns away.

She was so grateful for this second chance. If Wolfie felt

safe—which he clearly did—Abby could interact with her family in whatever way he felt so inclined.

She'd been worried that Wolfie would be traumatized, that he would associate Abby with being taken from her, that Abby would be a frightening presence in their home. But she could see that somehow, the opposite was true: Wolfie perceived Abby as a part of home. He didn't require an explanation. He didn't even miss a beat.

At first, she'd tried to explain it to herself: *they'd spent ten days together. They were so similar. They just clicked somehow.* She couldn't quite understand it, though. *How did Wolfie not fall apart in those ten days? How could he possibly, truly be okay?*

But underneath it was something less explicable, something that made her heart ache and her heart happy, simultaneously, and she decided that perhaps she didn't need to understand it, or pin it down with sentences and explanations: *somehow, they recognize each other.*

They just know how to be together, without words.

In all the ways she's tried to understand and pin down her family narrative over the last few decades, this mystery is the one she can lean in to, and accept.

Now, she's just about to go inside, when her phone beeps.

Bing.

Can I come to dinner with Abby?

Olivia frowns in disbelief. Hannah's lack of insight into how relationships work is dumbfounding.

You had an affair with my husband, Olivia replies. *What do you think?*

Later, Bing will send a barrage of text messages.

I can't believe you took him back!

He wanted to move in with me!

You should be grateful that I said no! If it wasn't for me wanting something better than your sad sack of a husband, you'd be single right now!

Olivia never receives them though. After she sends her response, as she slices mushrooms and onions, it occurs to her that she can just block Bing's number. Again. So she does.

When Nick and Charlie and her parents walk in the door a couple of hours later, she greets Nick with a warm kiss.

She squeezes Charlie's shoulder and hugs her parents hello.

"When will Abby be here?" Daniel asks, gruff and anxious. He looks old. Olivia clasps his hand gently.

"When he's ready," she replies.

GOOD GIRL BAD - EXCERPT

S.A. MCEWEN

A perfect life, or a perfect lie?

Rebecca Giovanni has a beautiful life—a job she loves, a new husband who's a great deal better than the old one, and two charming daughters from her first marriage.

It's hard not to be smug about how well she's done for herself.

She trusts her new husband.

Then she wakes to find him and her sixteen-year-old daughter missing. Their dog is dead, and the front door is wide open.

No matter what the police insinuate, Rebecca cannot believe Leroy and Tabby went anywhere together willingly. She's doing a stellar job, but blended families always have their difficulties. And they'd never leave the house without their phones and wallets.

But where are they? What happened in the house that night?

Rebecca's younger daughter is acting strangely, and her ex-husband is hiding secrets of his own—like where he was that night, and the real reason that he left Rebecca.

And Rebecca can't help thinking about the last time she saw her husband, and heard him say something she'd rather forget...

Monday

The house is silent.

Eerily so.

Rebecca Giovanni stands at the top of the small stairway to the kitchen. Below her, her sixteen-year-old daughter Tabitha's poodle, Charlie, lies on his side. He could nearly be sleeping, except he never sleeps in the kitchen, on the cold tiles. Rebecca can see that something is wrong, the position of his legs not quite right, his little head stretched back at an unusual angle, a rigidity about him sufficient information such that Rebecca does not go any closer; does not check.

Beyond him, the front door is wide open. A cold wind blows in from the street, through the leaves of the wisteria hanging lushly around the veranda, caressing Rebecca's forearms, swirling beyond her into the silent house.

The faint scent—her favourite flower—drifts past her toward the very back of the house, where her youngest daughter Genevieve is still sleeping. At fourteen, she is well and truly a teen when it comes to sleeping in. The house could fall apart around her ears and she would not so much as mumble a complaint.

It's spring—November—but still cold, and Rebecca shivers.

Leroy was not in their bed, and Tabitha was not in hers, either.

Rebecca's eyes roam around the kitchen.

She is not worried yet.

She notices Leroy's phone and wallet next to the fruit bowl; he has not gone far.

Tabby's phone, usually glued to her hand, is hanging precariously over the edge of the dining table. It looks like it should be falling, not balancing there.

But other than that, the house looks much the same as it always does when Rebecca gets up.

Rebecca is still not worried, despite the open front door, and despite the dead dog in her kitchen.

She's not worried yet.

But she will be.

Six Months Earlier

Rebecca smooths her Armani skirt across her thighs, a tiny, self-contained movement that she uses as a break in conversation. It makes her look calm and certain; it also soothes her when she needs to take a moment to think of what it is she wants to say.

It also reminds her of who she is: successful. Capable. In charge.

Rebecca doesn't speak rashly. She weighs her words up, her cool blue eyes resting on the recipient appraisingly. In this case, the recipient is Tabitha's home room teacher, Ms Paisley.

"I'm not sure what you're getting at?" she says eventually, her gaze unflinching.

Ms Paisley is young. Much younger than Rebecca, with kind brown eyes, which are right now blinking too frequently.

Nerves? Rebecca wonders.

She is used to people being nervous around her. Being wowed by her, in fact.

"Well, it's my first year teaching Tabby, of course," Ms Paisley responds, her words tumbling over each other in her haste to get them out. *It's probably your first year teaching, full stop,* Rebecca thinks to herself, patronising, but she keeps herself in check. "So I've only known her for a few months, obviously. It's just, she's always been one of our top students, and certainly her work earlier in the year was of a consistently high quality. It's just the last month or so that things have started to slip a little. Work not handed in, or not much effort applied, that kind of thing." She nearly looks apologetic, but seems to be trying her best not to. Even as Rebecca watches, she pulls her shoulders back and sits up a little higher in her chair.

"I'll have a word with her. But she's been her usual self at home. I haven't noticed any changes." Here Rebecca stops. *Typical,* she thinks. Just as she was taking ownership—"I" haven't noticed any changes—she spots Nate fighting his way around chairs and parents to reach them. Rebecca watches him silently. It's characteristic of her ex-husband to be late, and to look the opposite of calm and poised. Rebecca wonders if people think less of her because she was once married to him; if she's tainted by association.

"Sorry I'm late," he puffs as he comes to a halt beside them, casting about for a spare chair he can pull up. Spying one halfway across the room, he disappears again. Rebecca turns back to Ms Paisley, who looks as though she's very happy to wait for Nate to return.

Does no one have a sense of time and urgency except me? Rebecca thinks. If the roles were reversed, she would plough ahead without the late husband. She would say what needed to be said to whomever was present, and conclude the meeting decisively, precisely on time. Too bad, so sad if you were late and missed half of it.

She smooths her skirt again, the soft black fabric feeling expensive and luxurious under her touch. It clings to her thighs elegantly, ever so slightly suggestively, the muscle underneath nicely defined by regular weight classes and running. She raises her eyes to Nate again, her expression patient to anyone who didn't know her well.

To Nate, the patience is feigned, or mocking.

Here we are, waiting for you, again.

He seems unfazed though. He plonks the chair down next to Rebecca, and beams at Ms Paisley.

"How's my girl doing?" he says, and Rebecca has to stop herself from rolling her eyes.

"We're well past that, Nate," she says, cutting Ms Paisley off, and summarising the meeting so far, her demeanour crisp and business-like. She doesn't give Nate a chance to respond, but addresses Ms Paisley again with the air of someone who is used to making all the decisions.

"So, I'll have a word with her. I'm sure it's nothing to worry about. Tabby has always been a hard worker. If necessary, I can always limit her phone time. That's always rather motivating for her."

Ms Paisley looks surprised, and starts to open her mouth, but Rebecca cuts her off. "Did you have any questions, Nate?"

"Yes, actually," he says, though he knows full well that the question was rhetorical, designed to show Ms Paisley that they were co-parenting cooperatively. Rebecca didn't really expect him to say yes—to the point that she was half-rising from her chair, and stops mid-air.

She glances at Nate, something hard passing across her face so fleetingly most people would miss it, then she smiles and sits back down. Poised and gracious.

"Well, obviously we'll have a talk to her," Nate goes on, glancing at Rebecca. "But have you noticed anything at school that might explain it? Any change in her friendship group? Any boys she's hanging out with, that might be breaking her heart?" Nate looks like he is joking, making light of it, but Rebecca can see that he's just not sure how appropriate it is to ask Tabby's home room teacher about her love life, so he's disguising it under a protective, jovial father spiel.

Joke, joke, joke.

Rebecca thinks Nate is wasting his time. *Her* time.

Of course Tabby isn't seeing anyone.

Rebecca actively discourages relationships—she thinks Tabby is far too young, and has more important things to do. Like excel at school and get into university. The truth is, though, that Rebecca would have no idea if Tabby was romantically involved with anyone; they don't have that kind of relationship. Her certainty is rooted entirely in confidence that Tabby would not defy her wishes.

She's not worried by Ms Paisley's revelations. Tabby is strong-willed, and can be a little bit feisty, but she usually falls back into line when Rebecca flexes her parental rights.

"I very much doubt Tabby's been distracted by a boy," she says now, somewhat pompously, and Ms Paisley looks apologetic again.

"Well, actually, there has been a lot more socialising between the boys and girls this year, and I have noticed Tabby spending a lot of time with a particular young man, Trent Witherall. Has she mentioned him to you at all?"

Rebecca's demeanour shifts slightly, her posture stiffening, her jaw tensing. Nate glances at her uneasily.

"No, nothing," Rebecca says, her voice tight. She looks to Nate for confirmation, this time appearing genuinely interested in his response.

"She has mentioned Trent to me, yes," he says, directing his words to Ms Paisley. "But she's never made it sound like they're dating, or that she likes him in particular. His name has just come up a few times when she's talking about her friends, what they're doing on the weekend. Do you think they're...seeing each other?" Nate is aware of something simmering in Rebecca next to him, and he keeps his eyes carefully on Ms Paisley.

She, likewise, speaks back directly to Nate. "I would have thought so, yes," she says, but won't be drawn into why she thinks that. "I really think that's a conversation for you to have with your daughter, don't you think?" she hedges, and Nate wonders what she has seen.

Hand-holding?

Kissing?

Do kids kiss in the school grounds these days? He can't even remember how you woo-ed girls back in his day. He can't imagine his broody eldest daughter being billowed about by the strong feelings of young love.

But broodiness would be the perfect breeding ground for that intensity, that all-or-nothing consuming infatuation, wouldn't it?

Nate suddenly feels old and out of touch. Unlike Rebecca, he *has* noticed a change in his daughter. He would have said it had been much longer than this year though, and doubts very much it has anything to do with Trent Witherall. In fact, if his life depended on putting a date to it, he would have said it was a year or two ago that she started to become more withdrawn, more secretive. More broody.

About the time that Rebecca married that twerp, Leroy, in fact.

He steals a glance at his ex-wife. She is sitting very still, projecting that calm, reasonable, I-am-listening-to-you-deeply facade. He wonders if Ms Paisley can see through it.

He wonders what sort of man *can't* see through it.

What sort of man would fall for it.

He did, sure. But he was so young.

You can't put an old head on young shoulders, his father used to tell him, and he understands the saying differently now.

But Leroy is his age. Forty-five, give or take a few years.

What was Leroy's excuse?

Or was he just as stupid as twenty-year-old Nate?

And if Leroy was just as stupid as a twenty-year-old, what might have gone on between him and Nate's sweet sixteen-year-old daughter, that might explain the changes in her mood?

Back at home, Rebecca dumps her handbag on the kitchen bench with a loud thump.

She can hear chatter coming from the lounge room, the faint hum of the television, and she feels like storming up there and shutting it down, all of it. The television, the happy family time. Tabby has made her look stupid in front of her teacher, in front of Nate, but she's just glibly fooling around on a school night in front of the television without a care in the world.

"Tabby!" she shouts down the hallway, and there's a moment's silence, the voices quieting. Then the lounge door opens and Leroy and Tabby both emerge, padding down the long hallway toward her. They look so easy, so relaxed, and she feels resentful that she has to be the one to bring things back to order, to interrupt their fun, to remind them of the real world.

But somebody has to do it.

But just as she opens her mouth to say something cross, something biting, Leroy jumps clownishly down the five steps into the kitchen and grabs her in a dance pose, swinging her around, one arm firmly around her waist. He grins at her impishly.

"Look out, Tabby, Becci looks a bit peeved! What is it? An F? An expulsion? You've learned that Tabby's quit maths to do embroidery instead, and your dream of retiring on the back of your daughter's orthodontic practice have gone up in flames?"

He spins her around once more and then pushes her against the wall, kissing her bang on the lips in front of Tabby, his eyes laughing.

They'll have sex tonight, she can tell from his kiss, the way he holds her against the wall.

Her tummy flutters.

"Slipping grades," she squeaks, as she tries to wriggle out of his grasp, but the tension has gone out of her.

Leroy gives her a final smooch, then releases her. As he turns to go back to the lounge room, to give her space to chat to Tabby, no doubt, she thinks she catches a small smile toward her daughter, and a wink, and her stomach does less of a flutter, and more of a churn.

Monday

Rebecca shakes Genevieve roughly.

"Gen. Gen!" Genevieve groans, and tries to burrow back under her doona, but Rebecca is tugging it down harder and faster than she can pull it back up.

"Mum!" Gen protests, the cold creeping in from the hallway, from outside. From the situation in the kitchen.

"Where's your sister?" Rebecca's voice is urgent.

"Wha-at?" Genevieve rubs bleary eyes. "How should I know?"

It's now nearly 9 a.m. Two hours have passed since Rebecca found the front door open, and impatience and irritation have finally given way to something more urgent.

"Get up," Rebecca instructs her youngest daughter, rifling in her cupboard and throwing a tee shirt and some leggings at her. Genevieve holds them up in confusion. They're not appropriate for a Melbourne spring morning, no matter that's it's nearly summer. And they're certainly not appropriate for a school day.

"They're gone," Rebecca continues, looking through Genevieve's wardrobe like she might find some clue in there. "Leroy. Tabby. Leroy's car. But something's not right. I can feel it."

Hustling Genevieve through the house, shivering in the thin tee shirt Rebecca had handed her, she points to the mobile phones and wallets triumphantly. "See? Tabby would never go anywhere without her phone. And. Charlie." Here she glances at the little form underneath the sweater she had hastily thrown over him while she made phone calls, trying to find her daughter and husband.

Her eyes linger there, uneasily.

In her state of agitation, she completely forgets how one ought to break such news to anyone, especially to her teenage daughter.

Genevieve is still half asleep, and is struggling to make sense of her mother's words, which are being thrown at her, staccato-like. Bam. Bam. Bam. Bam. But when her eyes—following Rebecca's—fall on the shape under the sweater, she falls silently to her knees. She glances up at Rebecca, a question in her eyes, but she doesn't need a response, and her mouth gapes slightly, tears welling in her eyes, and she doubles over, a silent scream emanating from her open mouth.

She doesn't touch the sweater, just keens silently beside the little body on the floor.

Something about her daughter's grief shakes Rebecca out of her quest for an explanation. Genevieve is a thoughtful, sensitive, quiet teen, and Rebecca is surprised by the force of her pain.

No, that's not right. She's not surprised by the force of it—she's surprised that Genevieve is showing it, in public. To her mother.

Rebecca has her own pain about the dog, but it's been swallowed up by more important things, like where her husband and other daughter are, and why they left in such a hurry that they didn't even shut the front door.

She kneels beside Gen, putting her arms around her shuddering, small frame. "I'm sorry, I'm sorry," she whispers, mortified by her insensitivity. She holds Gen tight, keeping her close until her shaking slows and stills.

"What happened to him?" Gen hiccups, her voice painfully small.

"I don't know, sweetheart. But something's wrong. I'm going

to call the police. I've already called everyone who I can think of who might know where they are."

She'd been methodical—Tabby's friends. Trent Witherall's parents. Nate. The school.

Miss Ambrosia, the cafe where Tabby works on Saturdays —only to be told that Tabby hadn't worked there for over four months.

Where was Tabby going on Saturdays, then?

Where was she getting money from?

Rebecca mentally kicks herself. She'd looked into GPS tracking when she'd bought Tabitha her first smartphone. For a while, she'd obsessively checked her location, but Tabby was always exactly where she said she'd be. Even after that interview with Ms Paisley, when Rebecca was watching her closely, checking her location again daily—well, she'd gotten slack. She thought Ms Paisley had it wrong. Tabby was never over in Richmond, where Trent lived. She was always with her best friend, Freddy, studying, or else at work.

Rebecca had stopped checking. She really didn't think Tabby was the type to sneak around.

Now, though, she wonders what data she'd be able to access. Tabby's phone was right here. Didn't Google Maps keep data on everywhere you'd been? Was that true? And if it was, please dear God let Tabby's passcode be the same as it always was—the day she got Charlie, her twelfth birthday present. But he had arrived a week early, so it wasn't like she was using her *actual* birthdate, which Rebecca had told her a hundred times would be foolish, anyone could guess it.

Now, she grabs the phone off the table, presses the home button. Nothing. The phone is dead, and she scours around for a charger, usually lurking in every second power point, so many phones seemed to populate their home.

Personal phones. Work phones. Kids' phones.

Old, discarded phones.

Finally, she spies a cord hanging out from under the microwave, and plugs Tabby's phone in. It takes forever for even the little red battery symbol to blink on. Impatiently, she turns away from it.

"Did you know Tabby had quit Miss Ambrosia?" she asks Genevieve, trying to be gentle, but it's hard to keep the urgency, the accusing tone out of her voice.

The girl has pulled Charlie's stiff little body on to her lap. So different from Tabby, Genevieve is short and dark-haired, her brown eyes now staring vacantly into the distance. Charlie was Tabby's dog, but Tabby shared him generously with her little sister. She made sure to give Genevieve turns walking and feeding him, so the dog loved them both eagerly, joyously. Right above her, in fact, is an enlarged photo of the three of them. Charlie is clutched between the two girls, the love on their faces palpable through the camera lens. Tabby is crouched down—she's easily a foot taller than Gen. Her long, blonde hair is sun-bleached and messy, cascading over a slim, tan shoulder. Her blue eyes sparkle, staring right at you out from the wall.

Rebecca shivers. Leroy loves that picture. "Bottled joy" he called it, insisting that it was the one they frame, but it's always made Rebecca uneasy. Tabby looks older than she ought to in it. In a tank top and tiny shorts, she looks worldly, seductive. When she'd snapped at Leroy that perhaps that was why he liked it, he'd looked at her strangely. She still can't quite fathom the look that he gave her.

"They look like happy kids," he'd said, and she wondered if he could sense her jealousy. It wasn't as simple as the ageing mother envying the blossoming of youthful beauty. Rebecca herself was beautiful, she had no doubt and no insecurity about that. Tabby even looked a lot like her, really. Taller and slimmer, but their features were similar, their striking blue eyes.

No, it wasn't that. But it was hard to put her finger on the pang that the picture gave her, every time.

She wished she'd put her foot down, ordered a different print.

Now, though, she focuses back on Genevieve, who solemnly shakes her head.

Rebecca has no reason to doubt her. Gen has always been compliant, cautious, responsible. Tabby is more like her, Rebecca—impulsive, flamboyant. Sure of herself.

Or at least, she used to be.

Is she still flamboyant?

Things have changed, Rebecca knows that. But they've changed so slowly, so incrementally, that she hasn't paid that much attention. Now, though, she realises that the word *flamboyant* no longer applies to her eldest daughter.

Genevieve, on the other hand, seems to be plagued by self-doubt. She was never flamboyant, and Rebecca trusts her absolutely.

Rebecca casts her mind back to the Saturday just gone. Tabby had left on her bike at about 11 a.m. as she always did. She covered the lunch shift, making coffees and toasting fancy baguettes for a little cafe one suburb over from them. Or at least, that was what she was supposed to be doing. Rebecca was sure, in fact, that Tabby had boasted of a promotion not that long ago. Managing that shift. Definitely not more than four months ago.

So where had she been going every Saturday for four hours?

"Did you call Freddy?" Gen's voice is faint. Rebecca thinks that she hasn't grasped the seriousness of the situation. All she can think about is the damn dog. And the dog definitely needs thinking about, but right now, Rebecca just wants to know where Leroy and Tabitha are.

"Yes. I spoke to Fred. They haven't seen her this weekend. Freddy had already left for school by the time I called."

Fred and Frederica. For the hundredth time, Rebecca thinks *how vain. Silly*, even. To choose a name for your kid that's basically the same as your own. The amount of times there's been confusion over who is being referred to when you say "Freddy" is ridiculous.

Tabby and Freddy have been best friends since grade four, and Fred, the father, has promised he'll get Freddy to call Rebecca when she gets home from school, in case she knows anything. The way he says it makes Rebecca's stomach churn again.

In case she knows anything.

But Rebecca shoves that feeling aside and calls the police.

Monday

By the time Nate arrives, the police have already been at Rebecca's house for an hour.

A bored-looking officer stops him at the door, asking for identification and a reason for being there.

"My daughter is bloody missing with *that man!*" He has to stop himself from shouting the last two words, his voice rising unusually high.

Rebecca looks over at him, disdain written all across her face. Even disdainful, she's still a striking woman, with her aquiline nose and astonishing blue eyes. She's fitter than when they were together, too—always shapely, she's now toned as well, and her posture is that of a lioness, queen of her terrain.

The officer's ears prick up at Nate's tone, though. "We don't have any reason to suspect anything suspicious at this stage, sir," he says. "But can you tell me why you refer to Mr Giovanni in that manner?"

Nate can't though. He's never gotten along with Leroy, but do you usually get along with your replacement in the husband department? Leroy is too smooth, too handsome, and Nate is sure he'd be a player. The thought of him living with his teenage daughters is a constant thorn in his side. When Leroy had first moved in, he'd had to be very firm with Rebecca about some boundaries.

Leroy can't shower the girls.

He can't be in the bathroom with them.

At the time, they'd been ten and twelve, and Rebecca had just nodded and smiled sarcastically at him, but he could see how close she was to rolling her eyes. The girls didn't need any help in the shower, and Rebecca was clearly humouring him. But she didn't know men the way that he, Nate, knew men. Tabitha was a knockout. Even at twelve, men did double takes on the street. She looked like she was a model, with those long, lean, tanned legs and waist-length beach-blonde hair. She didn't look away, either. She'd fix those smouldering eyes on whoever stared, her face deadpan, neither shy nor embarrassed nor egotistical.

He often wondered what went on behind her eyes, but he never asked.

She was going to break hearts, though, and Nate would be damned if he'd let a grown man spend any time with her naked.

Now, though, he's forced to backtrack. Because what could he say?

The man would have to be blind to not ogle her, to not notice her in a sexual manner?

No. He was being ridiculous. He knew that. He was just paranoid. You hear so many terrible things these days. It was a terrible time to have a daughter.

To be a woman, he corrects himself. *It was a terrible time to be a woman. Or had it always been a terrible time, and now they were just starting to shout about it?* #MeToo had shaken him. And then there was the "incident" on Messenger. Here he cringes slightly, the police officer watching him curiously. It was all too difficult to think about, and he's whittled it down to a simple concept, one which was, however, impossible to enforce: *he did not want men thinking about his daughter in a sexual manner at all.*

Ever.

For the rest of her life.

Did all fathers feel like this? It was a constant mild panic, a sense of tension he could never quite shake. How dangerous the world might be for someone so beautiful.

He shakes his head at the police officer. "Nothing, sorry," he says. "I don't trust my ex's new husband, that's all."

"But it's just a gut feeling, isn't that right, Nate?" Rebecca interjects, her voice jeering at him ever so slightly. Nate ignores her.

"Is there any news?"

"Well, no one has been able to locate Mr Giovanni or Tabitha, but given there was no sign of forced entry, and Mr Giovanni's car is gone, it does suggest that he and Tabitha have gone somewhere together. We do understand that Mrs Giovanni feels that that is extremely unlikely, but at this stage, I'd suggest waiting until tomorrow to see if this all sorts itself out. These things usually do. Alternatively, if you want to file a missing person's report, we need you to come down to the station." The officer snaps his notebook closed with an air of finality, nodding to his colleague, a silent agreement that it was time for them to go.

"What about the dog?" Rebecca asks, her voice high. She has one arm wrapped around Gen, and Nate moves forward to give his youngest daughter a hug. He strokes her hair and pulls her head onto his chest, murmuring gentle words to her. Gen starts crying quietly again, but Nate can't tell if she's worried about Tabby or if she's crying for Charlie.

"Yes, the dog is concerning." The officer consults his notebook, as though that will help him clarify what has happened here, what the solution might be. But he doesn't add anything else, and Nate grits his teeth.

"What happened last night?" Nate turns to Rebecca, his voice tight. "Did you have a fight? With Tabby? With Leroy? How was she yesterday? Did she seem okay?"

Rebecca's face closes. "She was fine. Wasn't she, Gen? Except." Here she glances at the officers uneasily. "Apparently she quit her job months ago. But she's been pretending to go every Saturday like usual. Did you know that?" Her tone is accusatory, as though Nate being privy to something she wasn't privy to was the worst thing about that piece of information. She sounds defensive, *and so she should be*, thinks Nate. Saturday is Rebecca's day to look after the kids. *What else was she not keeping track of?*

Nate shakes his head slowly. "So where was she going?" he asks, his eyes conveying the challenge he would never dare to say aloud: *Why weren't you looking after her properly? Why weren't you paying more attention?*

But the police officer interrupts them. "We'll be off now. But do keep in touch and get back to us if they haven't turned up by tomorrow." He goes to hand Nate a card but Rebecca snatches it out of his hand, her eyes flashing. "Great," she snaps. "Just great. I'm telling you that things were tense between them."

This is news to Nate, and he looks up sharply.

"I am one hundred percent sure they wouldn't go off sightseeing together. Something is wrong, and isn't it your job to find out what?"

"Whoa, whoa, back up a minute," Nate interjects, nodding to the officers who are heading for the door, despite Rebecca's wrath. "Thank you, officers. We'll be in touch." He turns back to Rebecca. "What's this tension between Leroy and Tab? How long has it been like that? Did something happen?" He knows his suspicions are written all over his face, that Rebecca can see through him, can even probably anticipate the self-satisfied "I told you so" on the tip of his tongue, but he doesn't *want* it to be true. He wouldn't mind being right for once, in this particular relationship, but not about this. Despite his eager jumping on this news, he really does just want to find Tabby and check she's okay.

That she's not fooling around with Leroy, who even Nate has to admit is shockingly good-looking.

Sexy. Alluring.

"It's nothing." Rebecca stares back at him coldly. "He's just been really onboard with parenting her, and she resists it, you know? Says he's not her dad. Yada yada yada. Exactly what you'd expect from a sixteen-year-old toward her stepfather setting boundaries."

Nate studies his ex-wife carefully. There's something she's not telling him, but he can't guess what it is. *Is it a subtle dig, that he's not pulling his weight in the parenting department? That Leroy has had to take up the slack?*

"Where is Leroy on Saturdays when Tabby does her vanishing act?" he shoots back, and for a moment he sees a flash of doubt on Rebecca's face. She composes herself instantly though, looking at him pityingly. "My husband is not looking for any extracurricular entertainment, Nathan," she says archly. "We are extremely happy. If you want to know so much about what our daughter gets up to, perhaps you should do a little more with her yourself," and Nate winces, because it's true, he used to have the girls more, he used to have Tabby on Saturdays in fact, but things had come up, life had gotten in the way, and Tabby wasn't even home on Saturdays anyway, so what did it matter if they were at Rebecca's house just one extra day a week? He still had them two days a week, and for most of the holidays.

His thoughts are interrupted though, by a small sob from Genevieve, and Nate realises with a guilty start that he had forgotten she was even there, listening, and maybe Rebecca was right, maybe he *was* a shit dad.

Who would focus on making accusations rather than comforting their daughter?

"Hey, hey," he says, his face softening, and he reaches for Gen again, pulling her small, compact little frame into his arms. "Let's think about a funeral for Charlie, hey? We'll have it when Tabby's back. But we could make some plans, now. Maybe choose a tree to plant?" Nate's mind is working overtime. He's never been a fan of dogs, but he knows Genevieve is going to need a lot of support over this.

And also, he wouldn't mind taking her out of Rebecca's house and asking a few more questions about what she saw last night.

Not least because he might have been parked outside her house for a good portion of it.

ALSO BY THE AUTHOR

The Good Daughter

The Lost Boy

Good Girl Bad

Sister in Trouble

AUTHOR'S NOTE

When writing this book, I happened upon the media coverage of Sia's movie *Music* and the use of prone restraint in it. The scene was later removed, after protests from the autistic community, including a letter from a woman named Stacia Langley, which led me to the story of her son, Max Benson. Max was a thirteen-year-old autistic boy, who died in 2018 after being held in prone restraint at his school for an extended period of time.

Which led me to despair.

I work with vulnerable people. Sometimes I work with adults who were once vulnerable children. Show me a troubled adult, in fact, and I would stake my life on finding a thread back to trauma, in some form or another, as a child.

Children deserve our protection, our compassion, our respect.

If we want a compassionate world to live in, we have to start with children. Every. Single. One.

The majority of children who are restrained are disabled, black, brown, and very young. They often have a trauma history, and trauma changes our brains and how they function.

There are effective, evidence-based ways to work with trauma (I highly recommend *The Body Keeps the Score* by Bessel Van der Kolk), and they all start with compassion, not violence. Seclusion and restraint do not teach these children anything, except that the world is unsafe and traumatising, and adults, who are supposed to look after them, cannot be trusted to do so.

Not only does it not teach them anything, it also sometimes kills them.

You can find more information here: https://endseclusion.org/

ABOUT THE AUTHOR

S.A. McEwen writes nuanced and gritty psychological/domestic thrillers exploring relationships, especially within families... with a particular interest in how the dark gets in, and the complex things that drive us toward or keep us out of connection with each other

She is a qualified social worker and educator in youth mental health, and lives in Melbourne with two gorgeous boys and a puppy.

If you've enjoyed her writing, please get in touch and say hello! The links are listed below.

Get notified when I **release a new book** via my newsletter here: www.samcewen.com.

facebook.com/authorsamcewen

amazon.com/author/samcewen

bookbub.com/authors/s-a-mcewen

goodreads.com/samcewen

ACKNOWLEDGMENTS

To Stephanie—a million conversations with you will never be enough. Thank you for listening to my half-formed ideas, for alpha reading, for making suggestions on the social justice aspects, for the encouragement, and for the endless, endless laughs. You are the bestest thing.

To my beta readers—Sarah M, Amy Vox Libris, decillis, Kirsten Moore, Victoria Colotta—thank you for your thoroughness, your thoughtfulness, and your honesty. This is a much better book because of you.

To Erica Russikoff from Erica Edits—thank you once again for your brilliant editing, your attention to all the details, and your kindness with your edits. I am so grateful to have you on my team.

To Elizabeth Mackey for this beautiful cover—thank you.

And to all of you reading this book—thank you for taking interest in it. I really appreciate it, and I hope that you enjoyed it. x

www.ingramcontent.com/pod-product-compliance
Lightning Source LLC
Chambersburg PA
CBHW050155120726
47903CB00002B/638